Praise for Christopher Mouse

WINNER OF THE CALIFORNIA YOUNG READER MEDAL,
INTERMEDIATE CATEGORY

A TEXAS BLUEBONNET
MASTER LIST SELECTION

A BANK STREET CHILDREN'S BOOK COMMITTEE
OUTSTANDING CHILDREN'S BOOK OF THE YEAR

A *BOOK LINKS* LASTING CONNECTION

★ "The writing is nicely mannered but very accessible,
making the book not only fine for reading aloud
but also a delightful offering for children
moving past beginning readers."
—*Booklist*, starred review

"Christopher Mouse may be small, but he has
big adventures . . . His conversational account
of his life will delight young readers."
—*School Library Journal*

"Benson's highly textured, hatching-dense drawings
enhance the slightly period flavor . . . Christopher and his
brethren are engagingly and authentically portrayed."
—*The Bulletin of the Center for Children's Books*

"[A] gently refined tale."
—*The Horn Book Guide*

WILLIAM WISE

is the author of many books for adults and young readers, including *Ten Sly Piranhas*, illustrated by Victoria Chess; *Dinosaurs Forever*, illustrated by Lynn Munsinger; and the novel *Nell of Branford Hall*. He lives in New York City—in a nearly mouse-free apartment.

PATRICK BENSON

is the illustrator of such favorites as *Owl Babies* by Martin Waddell, *The Minpins* by Roald Dahl, and *Mole and the Baby Bird* by Marjorie Newman. He lives in the Scottish Borders with his family, including two guinea pigs, one hamster, one tortoise, two dogs, three fish, and two horses.

Christopher Mouse

The Tale of a Small Traveler

William Wise

illustrations by Patrick Benson

BLOOMSBURY
CHILDREN'S
BOOKS

To Yvonne Walther, Diane Arico, and Victoria Wells Arms,
three editors who, at different times and in different ways,
enabled Christopher Mouse to tell his story.

—W.W.

Text copyright © 2004 by William Wise
Illustrations copyright © 2004 by Patrick Benson
First published in the United States in 2004 by Bloomsbury Publishing
Paperback edition published in 2006

Published by Bloomsbury, New York, London, and Berlin
Distributed to the trade by Holtzbrinck Publishers

The Library of Congress has cataloged the hardcover edition as follows:
Wise, William.
Christopher Mouse : the tale of a small traveler / by William Wise ; illustrations
by Patrick Benson.
                    p.   cm.
Summary: After being sold to an unscrupulous pet store owner,
a young mouse lives with several owners and has many adventures,
before ending up with an appreciative family.
ISBN-10: 1-58234-878-2 • ISBN-13: 978-1-58234-878-0 (hardcover)
[1. Mice—Fiction. 2. Pets—Fiction.] I. Benson, Patrick, ill. II. Title.
PZ7.W77Ch 2004   [Fic]—dc22   2003056393
ISBN-10: 1-58234-708-5 • ISBN-13: 978-1-58234-708-0 (paperback)

Printed in the U.S.A.
6 8 10 9 7

Bloomsbury Publishing, Children's Books, U.S.A.
175 Fifth Avenue, New York, NY 10010

All papers used by Bloomsbury Publishing are natural, recyclable products made
from wood grown in well-managed forests. The manufacturing processes
conform to the environmental regulations of the country of origin.

Contents

Author's Note

It is a little-known secret that some small animals keep diaries of their adventures. Most often the animals are rabbits, hamsters, or white mice.

They hide their diaries in their burrows or cages. Sometimes the diaries end suddenly, and you wonder why. Did the small creature simply grow tired of writing and stop? Or did he come to an unexpected end—for good or ill? Most times, there's no way of telling.

I found Christopher's diary in a mouse hole, in the attic of a friend's house. Why it was there, I never learned. But I did read it—and if you read it too, you'll see how things turned out for him, small traveler that he was.

W. W.

1

AT MRS. CRIMMINS'S PLACE

My life began in the most commonplace way. I was born in an ordinary wire cage, on a soft bed of paper shavings. A few pieces of lettuce and a few lumps of cheese were strewn here and there.

At first my eyes remained shut so that I could not see anything around me. I slept most of the time, for I was very weak. I remember wondering why there was a rustling sound whenever I moved. But before long I grew so tired thinking about it that I fell asleep again.

Finally the day came when I was able to open my eyes. I saw the cage where I was lying and climbed unsteadily to my feet. Step by step I began to explore. I nosed around among the papers; I sampled the lettuce and the cheese; I drank from the round saucer that stood in the corner. The surface of the water cast a reflection. In it, I saw myself for the first time—my eyes, my nose, my fur, and my whiskers.

Then, one after another, I met four beings who looked like my own image in the water. They were my three brothers, and my sister, Anna. She was smaller than they were, and from the beginning I knew I liked her best.

When my mother saw that I was up and about, she began to explain things to me. "You are a white mouse like the rest of us," she told me, "and you will live in this cage for six or seven weeks—until Mrs. Crimmins comes to fetch you."

"Who is Mrs. Crimmins?" I asked her.

"She is the woman who owns us," my mother said. "In fact, she owns everything in this room— the food we eat, the cage we live in—everything."

"Do you like Mrs. Crimmins?" I asked.

My mother did not reply at once. She frowned and twitched her whiskers reflectively for several moments, and then I heard her sigh. "I suppose I like her well enough," she told me. "She *might* treat us worse than she does. Some owners are good—though I suspect not many of them—and some owners are wicked. I imagine—but I can't be sure—that Mrs. Crimmins falls somewhere in between."

Before I could ask her anything more, I heard a noise behind me. When I turned, I saw that a stout woman with bright red hair had come into the room. Mother told me it was Mrs. Crimmins, bringing us our food.

I'll never forget the first time she opened our cage to feed us. There was a long trapdoor at the top of the cage. She slid it back, and as she did, I heard a terrible grating sound that made the fur along my spine stand on end.

Her fingers appeared at the opening. They held strips of bruised lettuce and bits of yellow, moldy cheese. She dropped them into our cage, wriggling those fat fingers above our heads like five pale sausages. They were not a pretty sight to see.

Having given us the lettuce and cheese, she

dropped in our weekly treat—six well-salted mixed nuts. And they really *were* a treat for us. Many people think we dote on cheese, that it's our favorite food, but this simply is not true. Give any mouse a pecan or a walnut, an almond or a cashew, and he'll be extremely grateful. All mice have a passion for nuts, and that's the way to charm us if you should ever wish to.

I didn't know what to make of Mrs. Crimmins after that. Certainly the food she fed us most of the time was nothing to boast of—especially the cheese, which must have been considerably older than I was myself. And yet, she was not entirely devoid of kindness, for she also provided us with a weekly treat of salted nuts. Was she good—or was she not? I began to see why my mother had answered me so vaguely.

I thought a great deal about Mrs. Crimmins in the days that followed. If you are small and weak, and totally at the mercy of someone else, you have no choice but to consider the true nature of your owner; what she is like is extremely important to you.

As the days went by, I continued to observe Mrs. Crimmins whenever I could. And the more I did, the more I began to wonder about something my mother had said the first time she spoke to me. It was a remark that often troubled me as I wandered around our cage, or as I played with my brothers and sister among the paper shavings and strips of lettuce underfoot.

One day I decided I must know the answer. I came to my mother, who was sitting in a corner, and said, "You told me once that I would live here six or seven weeks—and then Mrs. Crimmins would come to fetch me. What did you mean when you said that? *Why* will she come to fetch me?"

I saw a startled look in my mother's eyes. A grave expression stole across her face. She pretended to be unconcerned, but my question had pained her. I had never seen her upset before. Suddenly I felt a pang of fear.

My sister, Anna, and my three brothers must have felt the same anxiety. They began to crowd around me, until all five of us were sitting in a half circle at my mother's feet.

She remained silent for a moment more. "Very well," she said at last. "I will answer your question. I suppose the time has come when you must know what lies ahead."

We nodded solemnly. Our usual playfulness had disappeared. It was clear that what she intended to say was important. It seemed equally clear that some of it could be rather grim.

2

"WHEN MRS. CRIMMINS COMES TO FETCH YOU"

"When Mrs. Crimmins comes to fetch you," my mother said, "your days in this room will be over. You will never return. I have lived here for a long, long time, and have had many more children than just the five of you, and if there's one thing I've learned by now, it is this: when Mrs. Crimmins comes with her cardboard box to take my children away, she takes them away for good."

The memory of her other children filled my mother's eyes with tears. To gain a little time to recover her composure, she turned and took a sip or two of water from the dish.

"But that is exactly as it should be," she went on. "When the proper moment comes, every young mouse must leave home and go out into the world to pursue his destiny. One day, Mrs. Crimmins will take you away. She will carry you off and sell you, either to a pet shop or a medical laboratory, for she is in the business of raising and selling white mice."

"Is it better to go to a pet shop," one of my brothers asked, "or to a medical laboratory?"

"It's *much* better to go to a pet shop," my mother said. "You aren't likely to stay there long. Before you know it, someone will come and buy you, and then you'll go home with your new owner.

"These days," my mother continued, "we white mice are considered very good pets. People love us for our energy and our antics, our pink noses and soft fur, our curiosity, and what some foolish souls are reputed to call our 'cuddlesomeness.' We are said to have winning ways, and accordingly we are generally well treated. Therefore—though happiness is often only a matter of blind luck—I think it safe to say that each of you will probably find great joy with the person who buys you for a pet and takes you home with him to live."

My sister, Anna, glanced in my direction before she said, "Must each of us go to a different home? Or could two of us have the same owner, and live together in his house for the rest of our lives?"

"I'm not sure about that," my mother replied. "I think most people buy only one mouse at a time. At least I've heard Mrs. Crimmins complain that owners don't buy enough of *her* white mice—so that's the conclusion I've come to. On the other hand, there must be times when somebody decides to buy two white mice, so they can live together and keep each other company. Yes, I suppose there's a good chance you and one of your brothers might end up in the same house, living together as you did here."

Judging from her expression, I knew this answer pleased my sister, and at first it had the same effect on me. Then I fell to thinking. Perhaps my mother simply had forgotten it—but what about the other possibility? Suppose one didn't go to a pet shop? Suppose instead . . . it was something I had to know.

"What happens," I asked, "if we are taken to a

medical laboratory? Would people come and buy us there too?"

My mother looked at me reproachfully, as though she wished I hadn't brought the matter up. Yet she did not hesitate. "No," she answered. "When a white mouse goes to a medical laboratory, he remains there all of his days, and the laboratory is the only owner he ever has."

"Does something bad happen to you there?"

"Sometimes. By no means always, though. Probably half the white mice in laboratories live splendid lives. They have plenty of companions, good food, and many diversions to keep them occupied."

"And the other half?"

"They are made the subjects of medical experiments," my mother said. "I'm not entirely certain what that means—for Mrs. Crimmins seldom has talked about it within my hearing—but I'm afraid that whatever it is, you are better off avoiding it. I think it must be the worst thing that can happen to a white mouse, next to having a wicked owner who mistreats you."

Our curiosity had been satisfied, and it wasn't long before the five of us returned to our usual activities. To all appearances, nothing had changed. We played once more among the paper shavings; we gnawed on bits of cheese and lettuce; we talked, explored, and kept as busy as before.

In reality, though, things were different now. An uncertain future hung over all of us like a cloud. My brothers put up a bold front. "No, indeed," one of them declared, "*I'm* not going to any medical laboratory. It's a pet shop, and only a pet shop, for me. And then a rich old man will come along and buy me, and after that I'll have a comfortable home and no end of salted nuts to eat for the rest of my life."

He grinned and swaggered about, and the other two soon joined him. They took turns boasting of the good luck they expected to have when Mrs. Crimmins came to fetch them. But beneath their bold talk and laughter they were as frightened of the future as I was myself.

I discovered that Anna feared the likelihood of our being separated from each other. "Do you think," she asked me one night, "that someone might buy both of us, so that we could stay together instead of going to different homes?"

"I think it very likely," I replied. "I'm not at all certain what will happen to the others, but this much I do feel sure of: somehow, you and I will always manage to remain together."

"I hope so," she said, "because you are the dearest to me of my brothers. I think my heart would break, Christopher, if we were to be parted and I had to say good-bye to you for the last time."

"That will never happen," I told her. "You'll see. We just need a little luck, and there's no reason why we shouldn't have it."

While awaiting the day of our departure, the five of us did not remain idle. One morning my mother announced that we were old enough to begin our schooling. "By the time I was your age," she told us, "I was studying my lessons so that I wouldn't leave home unprepared. My mother tried to teach me as much as she could about the world. Every mouse wants to do that for her children, and I can do no less for you."

She told us stories about her early life, before she

had come to stay with Mrs. Crimmins. She encouraged us to ask questions when we didn't understand, and was remarkably patient with us as long as we remained alert. If our attention wandered, though, we ran the risk of a sharp nip on the tail or a hard nudge in the ribs.

Besides telling us stories, she taught us to use the daily papers. Every other afternoon Mrs. Crimmins placed some clean pages of the *New York Times* or the *Post* on the floor of our cage. As soon as she left, my mother scurried around, examining columns of print, pictures, captions, and advertisements, to see what interesting facts they might contain.

"Anything in a newspaper," she informed us, "can be grist for a mouse's mill." At first she read the items aloud. There were stories about cars and airplanes, typhoons and hurricanes, baseball and football games, stray dogs and cats and other lost pets, and the arrival of the circus in town. Under her guidance we began to learn how to read for ourselves, using the huge letters in the advertisements. It wasn't long before we were familiar with the price of men's and women's clothing, the casts of the latest movies and plays, and the extraordinary bargains to be obtained at a Broadway restaurant that offered "All the Steak You Can Eat for $12.95!"

As our skills increased we took to reading the small print as well. Soon my brothers and I were devouring the sports pages, the comics, and any items about soldiers or space travel that we could find.

In this way, two or three weeks went by. Late one afternoon Mrs. Crimmins came and slid back the trapdoor. One by one she seized each of my three brothers, hauled him kicking and struggling out of our cage, and dropped him into a shoe box, the sides of which were punctured with airholes.

Anna and I huddled away in a corner, certain that it would be our turn next. Instead, Mrs. Crimmins said, "Three's enough for today," and slid the trap-door shut. It made its usual hideous noise, this time drowning out our cries of farewell.

That night Anna and I did little else but wonder about their destination. The next day, when Mrs. Crimmins brought us food and water, we heard her grumbling to herself. "That medical laboratory has a nerve! What do they think I'm doing here, raising white mice for the fun of it?"

Thus my sister and I learned about the others— that they had not gone to a pet shop as they had hoped, but to a medical laboratory. My mother, of course, had heard Mrs. Crimmins too, and for several hours she ran frantically back and forth inside our cage, scarcely able to restrain her anguish or conceal her tears.

3

LAST DAYS AT HOME

After that the time passed slowly for Anna and me. The emptiness of our cage reminded us of the others, and of the approaching hour when we ourselves would be carried away. One thought kept our spirits up: we had not yet been separated, and if our luck held out, we might remain together in the days to come.

With her other children gone, my mother became increasingly kind to us. She made sure we had the best paper shavings to sleep on; she urged us to eat the food Mrs. Crimmins provided. When we grew bored, she taught us new games to play. Our favorite was one called Nuts and Cheese. My mother said it was an ancient English game, invented centuries before by one of her innumerable ancestors while he was living in the Tower of London.

It didn't matter who went first. Anna, for instance, might say to me, "Cheese, Christopher, with the letter . . . G!" and as fast as I could, I'd answer, "Gruyère!" or "Gorgonzola!" Or she might say, "Nuts, Christopher, with the letter . . . *P*!" and I'd answer, if I could think of it in time, "Pecans!" Then, continuing in a circle, I'd test Mother for a cheese or a nut; next, she would test Anna; and finally we'd begin all over again with Anna and me.

A player lost a point for not answering fast enough. He lost two points if he made a mistake and answered with a cheese when he was supposed to answer with a nut, or the other way around. And he lost three points if he was challenged while testing and it turned out he didn't know the right answer. When a player lost ten points, the game was over, and the two winners would chortle loudly and sing:

Gadzooks, what a shame!
Gadzooks, what a shame!
Poor Christopher's not
Very good at the game!

No ifs and no buts,
We won in a breeze!
We beat him with nuts!
And we beat him with cheese!

Anna was quicker than I was, so at first nobody ever seemed to lose but me. I didn't enjoy that part of it one bit. Once, when they began to sing, I turned my back and refused to play anymore. Mother said, "Oh, Christopher, where *is* your sense of sportsmanship? We all must learn to lose graciously! Winning isn't what counts. It's knowing you've tried your best, and that everyone has had a good time—that's what is important."

The next day Mother lost the first game. She smiled serenely and said to me, "You see, Christopher, I'm not making a fuss, am I? No sulks, no tears. Winning doesn't mean that much to me."

She lost the next game, and her voice took on a slight edge. "I'm not implying that you did it deliberately, dear," she said to Anna, "but I believe that a few times you counted too fast on me. And Christopher—you used 'provolone' *twice*! I think perhaps we should clarify the rules on repetition!"

When—quite unaccountably—she lost the third game as well, she stifled a tremendous yawn and said, "I'm too sleepy to play any longer. Besides, Anna, if we're to enjoy the game, you mustn't count as fast as you've been doing today. And Christopher, 'Reindeer Cheese' was *not* fair . . . it was a trick . . . and that's the only reason I lost!"

"But I didn't think winning made any difference," I said. "I thought the important thing was to learn to lose graciously!"

A warning gleam appeared in my mother's eye. "Don't be sassy, Christopher. You know I don't like that."

"I didn't mean to be sassy," I said. "But now you're doing exactly what I—"

"Never mind what I'm doing, or what I'm not doing. I never told you to take *me* for an example.

Don't do as I *do*, do as I *say*! Well, I'm very sleepy. I'm going to take a nap for a while. When I wake up, we can play some more Nuts and Cheese if anyone feels like it, or we can play some other game."

Afterward I said to Anna, "Can you imagine? She made just as much fuss over losing as I did!"

Anna smiled and said, "I liked what she told us, though. 'Don't do as I *do*, do as I *say*!' I'm going to remember that, and when the time comes, I'll use it on my own children."

At night, when the room grew dark, my mother knew that Anna and I felt restless, and that fear of the future often made us uneasy. She talked to us soothingly and tried to teach us how to be more philosophical.

"Certainly the world *can* be grim at times," she told us once. "And yet, if we try, I think we can train ourselves to bear up under our burdens. Sometimes, when all of my children have left me and I'm feeling especially blue, I say to myself, "Never despair! How much worse the situation could be!'

"For instance, take the field mice—how dreadful *their* lives are. Twenty-four hours a day they're surrounded by enemies. Cats and snakes, hawks and weasels—some predator's always on their trail, hunting them down. When winter comes and food grows scarce, they often go hungry. And their living conditions! Rain or shine they're out of doors, their home a damp tunnel in the ground, or a drafty hollow in the corner of a barn. No safe, comfortable cage for them, inside a warm, familiar room!"

"All the same, isn't it better to be free?" I asked. "At least if you live in the fields, you don't belong to anyone. You don't have an owner, like Mrs. Crimmins, who can do whatever she likes with you."

"There are those who *say* it's better to be free," my mother conceded. "And yet, to scratch for a living all your life, or to go to bed hungry half the nights of the year? Well, I'm not sure freedom is the total delight some people claim.

"Besides, that sort of freedom is out of the question for anyone like us. Few household pets can live very long on their own. They don't know how to avoid their enemies. They don't know where to find food in the different seasons. As for a *white* mouse, why, our fur alone would be our undoing. Any half-blind cat can spot us moving a hundred feet off. So don't think you could thrive in the wilds like a field mouse, or prosper in the pantry like a house mouse. White fur would bring you to a cruel end—and it wouldn't take long."

"You mean, even if we *had* a chance to escape," my sister asked, "we shouldn't try to take it?"

"Escape," my mother answered gravely, "should be thought of only as a last resort. If you're sure your owner is either so careless or so cruel that your life is endangered, then you'll have no choice. Look for a hole in your cage, or some other way of gaining your liberty. Once outside, you must hope good fortune will smile on you, and that somehow you will survive."

She sighed and shook her head. "My great-uncle Julius tried to escape," she told us. "I remember hearing about it when I was young."

"What happened to him?" we asked.

"His owner was a traveling salesman who left him alone for a week at a time," my mother said. "Poor Uncle Julius was slowly starving to death. In desperation he managed to slip out, and for several days he lived on his own in the kitchen. Then tragedy struck."

"Did a cat find him?" Anna asked.

"No, he slipped and fell into a jar of strawberry jelly. Whether he died there from overeating, or drowned before he could climb back out, my great-aunt Flora never learned. He had his revenge, though. When the salesman came home, he decided to make a peanut butter and jelly sandwich—and there in the jar was my great-uncle Julius! They say the salesman's hair turned white in a matter of minutes."

My mother's sober expression grew more cheerful. "Fortunately, most owners are much better than the wretch who starved my great-uncle. And since they are, why shouldn't we white mice be content with our lot? To eat regular meals, to sleep in a warm, safe place—you could do much worse than that.

"And of course," she went on with a smile, "there's more to being a pet than just enjoying material comforts. With people for company, you'll never be bored. The things they say to their friends and relatives—and the *other* things they say when their friends and relatives have gone. Books? College? Listen to *people*, study them, and you'll end up with a real education!"

For several days we talked this way, and our conversations not only helped the time to pass but also kept Anna and me from thinking too much about our imminent departure. Because of this I was surprised one afternoon to see Mrs. Crimmins open the trapdoor and, instead of dropping in lettuce and cheese, put out her hand in my direction. Before I could dart away, her fingers closed around me. I felt myself lifted out of the cage. A moment later I tumbled down into the darkness of the cardboard box.

I landed on my feet and ran over to squint through one of the airholes. What would happen next? Would Anna come with me, or was I to set off alone?

I didn't have long to wait. In a few seconds the lid flew open, and my sister dropped down beside me. We had no chance to express our delight at still being together, for almost at once the box began to rise through the air and we felt ourselves being carried away.

The box rocked back and forth like a pendulum as Mrs. Crimmins strode from the room. Then all grew still while she placed the box on a table and put on her hat. Soon the violent motion started again. Peering out, I saw that she was carrying us down the front steps to the street.

It was hot inside the dark, swaying box, and I suppose that many a creature would have become seasick in such uncomfortable quarters. But a white mouse—though small and vulnerable—usually comes equipped with a strong stomach. Feeling no queasiness whatever, Anna and I dug our toes into the soft cardboard beneath us and prepared to endure the discomfort as long as necessary.

Our journey ended with a *thump* as Mrs. Crimmins put us down again. I heard a man ask, "What have you brought me today?" And our owner replied, "I've got two beauties for you, Doc."

My heart sank. *Doc!* What else could it mean, except that we were about to be sold to a doctor who worked in a medical laboratory?

I had no time to despair. The lid came off and a flood of light rushed in. Before my eyes could grow accustomed to the brightness, I was seized again, carried aloft, and thrust into another cage. Anna arrived soon after. I heard Mrs. Crimmins say, "Well, how do you like them?"

"Just so-so," the man said. "They look kind of small to me."

"Not small," Mrs. Crimmins protested. "They're *young, young.* Hardly a month since they were born! And top grade, best quality. I'm asking five dollars apiece."

"I might give you a dollar each."

"You can't be serious!"

"Okay—say two dollars apiece."

"That's outright thievery!" Mrs. Crimmins cried. "I've pampered them like no other mice I've ever raised. I've fed them on nothing but the finest Liederkranz, the freshest lettuce, and I've been doing it for six or seven weeks! Just think of my expenses!"

"I thought you said they were '*young, young,* hardly a month since they were born!'"

"Make it four dollars each?"

"Two dollars fifty each. That's my top price."

Anna and I, crouching in our cage, dazed by the journey and awed by our new surroundings, watched as the money changed hands. What a disagreeable experience it was, to see ourselves bought and sold. Nor was it pleasant to realize how little we were worth—much less than "all the steak you can eat" in a Broadway restaurant.

Mrs. Crimmins was not pleased by the transaction either. I saw her standing near the front door, scowling, her red face even darker than usual. Then the door opened, a bell tinkled overhead, and she was gone.

No sooner had she left than Anna said to me, "That man over there in the white coat, Christopher—she called him 'Doc.' Does it mean we've been sold to a medical laboratory?"

"I'm not sure," I said, "but I intend to find out." I looked around the room. It was filled with numerous birds and animals, some running, some standing, some sleeping in one of the corners of a cage.

"Hello there," I called out to a large, brightly colored bird with an enormous beak. He was sitting on a swing inside a cage labeled PARROT. "Where are we? What kind of place is this?"

"A madhouse! A perfect madhouse! HAW!"

"No, I mean, is 'Doc' a doctor, and is this a medical laboratory where they do experiments?"

"Experiments? All life is an experiment, as the Great Poet once said. HAW!"

Above us someone called out from a cage labeled HAMSTER. "Don't pay any attention to *him*. He enjoys being silly—*and* rude."

"Well," I said, "can you tell me, please, where we are?"

"Pete's Pet Shop. Pete was the owner, you see, but he got sick and Doc bought him out. Doc isn't really a doctor—that's just his nickname. And he isn't very nice, either. For one thing . . ."

I wasn't listening anymore. Anna had heard everything; now she put her cheek against mine and said, "At least we're not in a laboratory, where they might use us for experiments." With that she burst into tears, but only to prove—or so she claimed later—how happy she felt at our amazing good fortune.

RUSSIAN
HAMSTER

WHITE
MICE

PARROT

CHAMPION

BETA

4

POEMS AND PARTING

It didn't take us long to settle into our new life at the pet shop. At first there seemed to be nothing but confusion; our ears were constantly deafened by the birds chattering in their cages and the puppies barking as they played in their pens. But after a while things began to sort themselves out, and within a day or two Anna and I felt as much at home at Pete's as we had at Mrs. Crimmins's place.

We soon discovered the rules of pet shop life. During the day, everything is business. You keep your eye on each new customer, from the moment the bell rings and he enters the store. What is he like?—that's the crucial question. Would he make a kind, generous owner? If you decide yes, then you hope he will come by and look into your cage, and perhaps buy you for himself. But if his face is hard and cruel, his voice sharp, his eyes cold and shifty, then you hold your breath and hope against hope that he will pass you by.

At night, after the shop closes, life takes on a different flavor. The lights are off, the customers gone, and for a few hours one's anxiety about the future comes to a halt. The chattering of the parakeets grows less shrill, and the canaries' single notes become more harmonious. The puppies play less frantically until at last, overcome with weariness, they curl up in their pens and fall asleep. Some of the older birds and animals begin to reminisce about the various places they've been and the things they've seen.

The Parrot was a great talker. His cage was on one side of ours, so it was easy for Anna and me to engage him in conversation. Sometimes we were joined by the Hamster, who lived above us on a higher shelf.

Both the Parrot and the Hamster were what is

known as "Retreads," which means that they already had been in a pet shop, and had lived in a number of homes in the outside world. Now they were awaiting the day when they would be bought again and carried away by a new owner. Most of the inhabitants of the shop were not Retreads but, like Anna and me, were what was referred to as "First-timers" or "Freshmen."

The Parrot had lived for several years in Greenwich Village. "My Bohemian period," he said to us one night. "The best years of my life—for, without doubt, my owner was an extraordinary artist, a brilliant poet, a towering and original genius. He enjoyed having me perform at parties and taught me to recite all sorts of things: his puns and riddles; his quips, sallies and ripostes; and, of course, some of his poetry, which was absolutely— he said so himself—the most brilliant intellectual achievement of the last five hundred years."

The Hamster seemed unimpressed. "Why don't you tell them the man's name?" he asked in a sour voice. "Otherwise they might think you mean William Shakespeare."

"It will be a pleasure," the Parrot said. "My owner's name was Schwartz—T. S. 'Howling Mad' Schwartz, he called himself—'The Greatest Poet of Them All.'"

"Would you recite some of his things?" Anna said. "We'd love to hear them."

"Perhaps *you'd* love to hear them," the Hamster said.

Ignoring the Hamster, the Parrot cleared his throat several times, croaked "HAW, HAW" to himself once or twice, and said, "I'll give you an example of his riddle-and-pun combination. Here's one that always went over big at parties. I quote from the Master: while he was in an especially bad temper, what did the Dead End say one night to the Cul-de-Sac?"

"I'm sure I have no idea," Anna replied.

"You aren't supposed to," said the Hamster. "If you knew the answer beforehand, what would be the point of the question?"

"But why do you keep interrupting?" I asked impatiently. "What *is* the answer?"

"The answer is," said the Parrot, "that while in an

especially bad temper, the Dead End said one night to the Cul-de-Sac, 'We are not a mews!' "

There was a good deal of confusion after that, and some spirited quarreling between the Hamster and the Parrot. They both tried to explain what "Cul-de-Sac" meant, as well as "Dead End" and "mews," and then each began to talk excitedly about Queen Victoria, and what the point of the joke was—so that by the time Anna and I understood what the joke had been, everyone was thoroughly sick of riddle-and-pun combinations.

"Maybe his poetry would sound better," Anna finally said to the Parrot, who was sitting in offended silence on his perch. "If you can remember any, would you recite us some?"

"He can't recite it for you if he *doesn't* remember," said the Hamster. "He'll talk your ears off with it, if you give him the chance."

"If it were merely my own poetry," the Parrot said, "I would remain silent. But I feel the work of the Master belongs to the world. Let me see—here is a poem I believe you might enjoy. It's called 'The Waistband,' because it's all about food and eating. Or at least it appears to be, though of course one can't really be sure what a poem's about if it's a masterpiece. This is how it goes:

> Let us go then, thee and me,
> Where the menu is spread open on the knee,
> Like a pancake, buttered on the table.
> Let us go—"

"Let us *stop!*" cried the Hamster in a shrill voice. "You may have lived with a poet, but I've lived with a critic for more than a year, and I know what poetry *is*, and what it isn't! If you can't do better than that, you should keep silent. Altogether silent!"

"*Altogether silent!*" the Parrot mimicked. "What felicity of language. What elegance of phrase. What rot! HAW! As a poetic genius whose name I won't mention once remarked, 'The only good critic is a dead critic!'"

"I wish you'd try again," Anna said. "Perhaps another of his poems—but maybe not a masterpiece this time."

The Parrot ruffled his feathers and hopped down

to the floor of his cage. "I'm deeply offended. Almost too deeply to go on." He gnawed morosely on one of the bars and said, "Very well, just for you, my dear, because you're young and eager to learn. Here's "To a Lady on Wearing a Hat Which She Shouldn't.'"

"Some grammar," the Hamster muttered.

> *"Those feathers in your hat, I fear,*
> *Will make you look too fat, my dear.*
> *So why not try some other props?*
> *Perhaps a bag of lemon drops!*
> *Or else fresh parsley in a spray,*
> *This year it's being worn that way.*
> *But if you don't mind looking fat,*
> *Just leave the feathers in your hat!"*

Anna and I liked the poem, but of course the Hamster didn't. He made some cutting remarks about rhythm, rhyme, and meaning, and there was another bitter quarrel. The Parrot fell silent and refused to recite again, though Anna begged him to. In a grudging voice he said, "Well, perhaps another time. Maybe tomorrow night, if you can promise me we'll have no more of the crude, rude, and repulsive interruptions that we've had tonight."

As things turned out, there never was a second recital. The next afternoon a woman came into the shop with her daughter. Anna and I studied them closely, and we decided they might make good owners. Our hearts beat faster when we heard the woman say to Doc, "Angelica Rose thinks she wants a white mouse."

"Step right over here," Doc said. "I've got a couple of beauties I'm sure your little girl will like. They're big and fat—raised on nothing but the finest lettuce and the best imported Liederkranz cheese!"

The woman peered at us through the front of the cage. "They look kind of cute," she said. "How much are they?"

"Five dollars and fifty cents apiece—eight seventy-five for the pair."

"Oh, she wouldn't want two," the woman said. "Just one would be plenty. Angelica Rose, dear, you know how you're always changing your mind. Are you *entirely* sure you want a white mouse?"

"Of course I'm sure," the little girl said.

"All right, we'll take one," the woman told Doc.

"I'll get a box for you right away," Doc said.

Anna and I looked at each other, and for several moments neither of us spoke. "They both seem very nice," I finally said. "If it's you they pick, I know you'll be happy with them."

"Yes, they do seem nice," she said. "But it doesn't matter much, does it—since both of us will be going off alone."

"Doc's coming with the box now," I told her.

"Don't forget me, Christopher."

"How could I forget my own sister?"

I could see Doc standing by the cage. "Strange things happen," I said. "Maybe someday we'll be back together again."

"Maybe someday."

"Good-bye, Anna."

"Good-bye, Christopher."

The cage opened, and Doc said, "Which one do you want, Angelica Rose?"

"That one!" the little girl said, pointing at Anna.

Doc opened the cage wider and reached in to catch her. I shut my eyes and didn't open them for a long time—not till after the shop bell had stopped ringing and I knew that the woman and her daughter had carried Anna away.

5

FREDDY WILLIS

With Anna gone I sank into listlessness and depression. It was painful to realize how unrealistic our hopes had been, and even more painful to admit that I'd been a fool.

Life at the pet shop had lost its zest. I scarcely bothered to eat; I was bored by conversation. My friends tried to cheer me up, the Parrot by offering to recite the most notable poems of T. S. "Howling Mad" Schwartz, the Hamster by proposing a lecture series on the techniques of modern literary criticism. I declined them both. I went to sleep at an early hour and rose reluctantly, long after the lights had come on.

Even when new customers entered the shop, I felt no curiosity about them. But because I had nothing better to do, I continued to observe them as they passed in front of the fish tanks and the cages. From force of habit I divided them as skillfully as I could into "kind" owners and those who would be less satisfactory.

One morning not long after Anna had been taken away, I heard the bell ring and saw a dark-haired boy enter the shop alone. The Hamster began to quiver with excitement. Children rarely have enough money to buy puppies or parrots, but sometimes they do have enough to buy a hamster or a mouse.

"That boy is no mere browser," the Hamster called down to me. "Keep your eye on him. He's come here to buy one of us, I can feel it in my bones. See how he keeps putting his hand in his coat pocket? That's probably where he's carrying his money."

"Well, I don't think too much of his looks," I replied. "Did you ever see such a scowl?"

"He may be nearsighted—that can make people

frown," the Hamster said. "Or maybe he's nervous—children frequently are when they go into a strange shop. Better wait for his smile before you make up your mind. A smile's often the most valuable clue of all."

The Parrot hopped on his swing and, knowing that he himself was not likely to be chosen, croaked with good-natured mockery, "Perfectly true! A valuable clue! HAW!"

His voice made the boy turn in our direction. As he caught sight of us, his mouth fell open. At the same moment, he gasped with delight. "Oh, you're just what I want!" A smile lit his face—the most radiant smile I'd ever seen.

"You were right," I said to the Hamster. "He must have been nervous. He'd make a good owner, don't you think?"

"The best that's come in yet," the Hamster said. "I hope I'm the sort of pet he has in mind. He'd suit me perfectly—and as an old Retread, I know what I'm talking about!"

The Hamster's hopes soon disappeared. Without a second glance at him the boy rushed forward and stared into my cage. *So I'm the one you like*, I thought. *Well, I suppose if you have enough money, in another few minutes I could very well be yours.*

I felt no joy at the discovery. Since Anna had gone, I no longer cared about the future, for I had convinced myself that it could not hold anything promising.

Still smiling, the boy continued to stare at me. I heard the Hamster sigh and say in a melancholy voice, "*You're* the one he wants. Bad luck for me— good luck for you. Congratulations!" The Parrot, showing extraordinary tact, remained silent.

After a while the Hamster called out, "Christopher, what's the matter with you? The boy is here to buy a pet. Don't stand there like a statue—you've got to respond! Show some animation, verve, *esprit de corps*! Do you want to lose the chance of a lifetime?"

He was right—I knew it at once. I began to go through my paces with as much enthusiasm as I could muster; I trotted up and down, pretending to be lively and eager. I nibbled a fragment of stale cracker and drank water from the dish. Then I trotted around again, putting on what I hoped was a convincing display of energetic and appealing activity. After all, a kind owner is better than a mean one—and who wants to live forever in a pet shop?

I was hard at it when I caught sight of Doc coming across the room. "Ah-ha," he said. "Young man, are you interested in purchasing this fine, pedigreed white mouse?"

The boy nodded timidly. "Yes—if he's not too expensive."

I shuddered when I heard his voice. He sounded so shy and uncertain compared with Doc. *Oh dear, I told myself, this is going to be awful . . . .*

"Well," Doc said, "how much were you planning to spend? This particular shipment of white mice came from the West—all the way from Oregon—priced at ten dollars apiece. But since there's just the one left, I've marked him down considerably."

"I have only seven dollars to spend," the boy said.

"And some people don't believe in coincidence!" Doc cried. "Seven dollars is *exactly* the new price! I'll tell you what I'll do: because I see you're a nice young man who will give this top-grade animal an A-One home, we'll forget about the extras—the state tax, the city sales tax. I'll pay them out of my own pocket. By the way, have you got a cage to keep him in?"

"Yes, thank you," the boy said. "I already have one."

"Then I'll find a carrying box, which I'm going to give you free of charge. After that we'll call the transaction completed, and the sale bona fide and down in the books!"

The Hamster said, "Doc must be getting soft. A free box? He used to make the kids pay for them with their lunch money!"

"Mice are best when they come from the West!" the Parrot croaked. "All the way from Oregon! HAW! It's piracy on the high seas, shipmates! Welcome to Captain Blackbeard's Pet Shop! You pays your money here, and you walks the plank!"

Doc had disappeared into a closet at the back of the store. While he was gone the boy peered at me and said, "You're a fine little fellow, aren't you? Your fur's so white, and your nose is so pink. You'll like it once we get home!"

He was smiling again, the poor kid. Seven

dollars—such a ridiculous price to pay. Ah well, as I'd heard the Hamster declare more than once, a fool and his money are soon parted, especially when there's somebody like Doc around to do the separating.

I must confess that I felt contemptuous of my new owner as he carried me out of the shop. What a simpleminded boy he seemed to be, letting himself be swindled out of his few dollars by Doc, without a murmur of protest or, what was worse, without the slightest suspicion that the pet shop owner had taken advantage of him.

On the way home, however, I began to wonder if I weren't underrating him. He carried me for a block or two, and then we took a bus for fifteen or twenty blocks more. Every second of the journey he held the box carefully, in a manner far different from that of Mrs. Crimmins. It was clear that he was concerned about my well-being and wished to have me jostled as little as possible. Perhaps, "though not outstandingly gifted intellectually," as the Parrot or the Hamster might have said, he was the sort of thoughtful boy who would make an admirable owner.

I discovered during the next few days that my second thoughts had been justified. Frederick Willis—everyone called him Freddy—was good natured and generous. Apparently I delighted him, and he was determined I should be the happiest white mouse in the city of New York.

Nothing was too good for me. He spread out soft, fresh paper shavings at least twice a week and filled the water dish faithfully, morning and night. My long, spacious cage was placed by the window. Through the panes I could watch the traffic below, and I never felt lonely when I was by myself.

Before buying me, Freddy had gone to his neighborhood library and taken out a book containing a chapter on the proper care and feeding of white mice. He had learned that we do not enjoy being in the sun too much. I was hardly there an hour before he placed a small homemade cardboard house beside me. This gave me a place to retreat to whenever the sunlight fell directly into my cage.

Freddy had two younger brothers, Mike and Pete. They were interested in me from the moment I arrived. At first I was terrified they might handle me too roughly if given the chance, but Freddy settled the matter at once.

"This is the way you must pick him up," he told them firmly. "And be sure you do it very gently!"

Every evening when Freddy came back from school, I was let out of my cage and allowed the run of his room. At such times he shared me freely with his younger brothers; one moment I'd be climbing his arm, the next I'd be climbing Pete's or Mike's. Sometimes I ran around the desk and examined the pile of sports magazines, the pencils, and the box of paper clips. If the drawers were left open, I'd dive in and explore them, while outside I'd hear the three boys saying things like, "Where is he?" or "I just saw him!" or "You don't think, Freddy, he'll get lost in there?"

My owner was marvelous when it came to food. "How will you know what he likes to eat?" Pete asked.

"The book says all mice like cheese," Freddy told him.

"Yes, but what kinds of cheese?"

"We'll find out—scientifically," Freddy replied.

Each day he brought me two kinds of cheese and watched to see which one I ate first. After several weeks he knew I was partial to Liederkranz and Camembert, and that a good French Brie, if sufficiently soft and runny, was always my first choice.

One night he returned from the library in great excitement. "This new book," he told Pete and Mike, "says that mice in captivity would rather eat nuts than cheese! Maybe we've been on the wrong track! Maybe we'll have to start the experiments all over again!"

Can you imagine my delight when he opened a can of mixed nuts and, along with a wedge of Brie, thrust in half a walnut? "Which do you think he'll eat first?" Freddy asked his brothers.

"The cheese," said Mike.

"The cheese," said Pete.

"I wonder," mused Freddy.

They weren't kept in suspense for long. That half walnut disappeared so fast you would have thought there were ten half-starved mice inside the cage instead of only me.

"Did you see that?" Freddy said. "The book was

right! He does like nuts better! You know what we'll do? We'll go through the whole can till we learn which kind's his favorite, and after that we'll feed him nothing else!"

It was typical of Freddy. He enjoyed making other people happy; he liked to know that somebody else was pleased. And yet, I've heard it's possible to be *too* generous. I think Freddy was. He found it difficult to disappoint anyone. I guess it made him feel so bad himself. Because of this—and my own stupidity—something happened that no one could have foreseen.

6

THE ORPHAN BOY

As a mouse grows older, experience teaches him to be wary of the future, to take nothing for granted about the days to come. Often the best time to exercise caution is not when the heavens already have grown dark, but when there isn't a threatening cloud to be seen in the sky. That's the moment to haul in sail and make certain everything aboard is sturdy and shipshape. For beyond the horizon a storm may be gathering, and if it should catch you unprepared, it may swamp your frail craft and in a single instant sweep your good fortune away.

I was still too young to realize how easily my world could be turned upside down. Life with

Freddy was extremely pleasant, that much I knew. I enjoyed comforts and luxuries—more, I was sure, than most white mice ever enjoy. I was unlucky in only one respect: I did not understand how precarious my position was.

I grew careless about pleasing my owner; I assumed I would always be indispensable to his happiness. When he tried to teach me tricks, I made no effort to learn them. At night, when he let me out to exercise, I was as friendly to his younger brothers as I was to him. Impartiality was not wise. I should have scampered along the arm of Freddy's sports jacket with extra enthusiasm, reminding him of my gratitude and affection. I didn't, and that was one of the reasons the unexpected event took place.

It was Saturday morning, and I lay half in and half out of my cardboard house, nibbling on the remnants of a hazelnut while I tried to decide whether to curl up and go to sleep or take a run around the cage. Freddy came in with a new friend. He was a blond, blue-eyed boy named Aubrey Sharpe III who lived in a nearby apartment house. He and Freddy, I learned, had met a couple of Saturdays before at the public library, where they both had gone to return some books. It was his first visit to Freddy's room.

As soon as Aubrey saw me, he stooped over and stared into the cage. "What long whiskers he's got!" he said to my owner. "And such beautiful white fur! He's terrific! No wonder you don't want to trade him."

"Of course I don't," Freddy said.

"If I were you, I wouldn't want to trade him either. Not even for a pocketknife like mine."

"I *did* like your knife," Freddy said. "But I wouldn't trade him—not for anything."

"I know you wouldn't. Why should you? He's better than any knife *I've* ever seen."

"You bet he is," Freddy said.

"Of course, once he's dead, you won't have anything left—and I'll still have my knife, the way I do now."

"What do you mean, 'once he's dead'?"

"Well, he *is* a pretty old mouse," Aubrey said. "You can tell by the length of his whiskers. If he were young, they wouldn't have had the time to grow that long."

"I never thought about his whiskers," Freddy said. "All the same, he's my pet and I'm going to keep him."

Aubrey had taken the knife out of his pocket. He opened one of the blades. As I watched him, I couldn't help being amused. He was a shrewd one—making up all that nonsense about my whiskers. But I was certain his tricks would do him no good. Freddy liked me too much. I was his prize possession. He wouldn't part with me under any circumstances.

"It's made of the best-quality steel," Aubrey said. "The one blade's got a slight nick, but otherwise it's practically brand new. And the can opener's important, for times when you're lost in the woods and have only a can of beans to eat and would starve otherwise. Here, take another look at it, Freddy."

The knife was handed over. Freddy shut and opened the blades and tested the edge of the largest one on his forefinger. His admiration was intense, and for a moment I felt a rush of panic as I saw him wavering. Then he shook his head and handed the knife back to Aubrey Sharpe III.

"It's okay," he said. "But I could never do it. I could never trade my pet for anything."

How foolish of me to have had any doubts! Dear, good Freddy—what an owner he was! I took another nibble of the hazelnut and munched on it complacently.

Aubrey dropped the knife back into his pocket. "I don't blame you," he said. "A pet shouldn't be traded. If I had a pet myself, I might give him to a friend, just to make my friend happy, but I'd never trade him. Not for anything."

"Don't you have a pet?" Freddy asked him.

Aubrey shook his head slowly and lowered his eyes. "No, I don't," he said. "In fact, to tell you the truth, Freddy, I've never had one in my entire life."

"You've never had even one? But that's awful, Aubrey. How come?"

"Mom and Dad have always been very strict with me. They told me if you have a pet, it's bound to mess up the apartment. So they said I'd have to wait some more, till I was old enough to take care of it all by myself."

"Maybe if you ask them now, they'll let you have one."

Aubrey sighed and looked away. "Now it's too late," he said. "Pets cost money, and we haven't got any money left."

"But your dad must have some, or you couldn't live in a big apartment house."

"We'll probably be moving soon," Aubrey said with another sigh. "I'll tell you a secret, Freddy, if you promise not to tell anyone. My dad's lost everything. It's called going bankrupt. Any day now they'll be coming around to take away our furniture, and the dishes, and our TV. And they'll probably arrest Dad and put him in jail, and maybe Mom too. Then I'll have to live somewhere else—I guess most likely in an orphanage. And you know, in an orphanage, they don't let the children have any fun, or give them money to buy pets, or anything like that."

I thought Freddy was going to burst into tears. The tragic tale had affected me as well. Poor Aubrey! Never had a pet, and now the orphanage looming ahead of him! I was so busy commiserating with the unfortunate boy that I hardly noticed the change in Freddy's expression. Suddenly he was smiling, his face as beautiful, as radiant as I'd ever seen it.

"Aubrey, do you know what I'm going to do? I'm going to give him to you! Not trade him—just give him to you, because you're my friend, so you can have some fun when you go to the orphanage!"

Things were happening too fast for my brain to keep up. My first thought was, *How generous of Freddy, what a marvelous thing to do!* Then it struck me: *hold on, that's* me *he's talking about. That's* me *he's being so generous with. He's handing me over to somebody I've never seen before, an utter stranger—and somebody he doesn't know so well himself. How can he be sure I'd like it with Aubrey, or that I'd be happy living in an orphanage?*

"Are you giving him to me for keeps?" Aubrey asked. "I mean, I might not be going there right away. . . ."

"Sure it's for keeps," Freddy said.

Aubrey took out a handkerchief and blew into it loudly. "Gosh," he said, "nobody's ever been so nice to me. You're a *real* friend, Freddy. And I'll take good care of him. He probably won't live very long because he's so old, but I'll do everything that I possibly can for him because he's the only pet I've ever had."

Freddy told him what foods I liked to eat and gave him instructions for keeping my living quarters tidy. Aubrey thanked him again and picked up the cage. Together they brought me down to the street and began to walk up the block toward Aubrey's building.

"Can I come around once in a while?" Freddy asked, "and see how he is?"

"I wish I could let you," Aubrey said, "but Dad and Mom are so ashamed of not having any money, they've told me I can't invite my friends over. We could talk on the phone, though. You see, we can't tell at home what's going to happen next. Maybe the police are there right now. Or maybe today, the furniture's been taken away."

"Going bankrupt must be terrible," Freddy said.

Aubrey nodded solemnly. "It is. But knowing I've got a true friend makes all the difference. I'll see you around, Freddy."

To my bewildered eyes, Freddy Willis turned and disappeared, walking back toward the familiar room I had come to know so well. The ideal owner, gone—and with such swiftness. I could hardly believe it had happened. And here I was, in a strange elevator, riding up with another boy whom I scarcely knew.

I consoled myself with the thought that I was the first pet Aubrey had ever had. Therefore, I would be particularly important to him. Surely he would treat me with kindness, and even at the orphanage would he try to provide me with some of the luxuries to which I had lately grown accustomed.

Such was my reasoning as we entered the dining room. I saw that Aubrey's father and mother were finishing their lunch. At least they still had food to eat, and the furniture and dishes hadn't been taken away. And as far as I could see, there was no sign of the police, either.

"Aubrey, what have you brought in this time?" his mother asked.

"Just a white mouse," he said.

"I thought you were keeping turtles these days."

"I was. Till I found a way to trade them off last week."

"And the garter snake? And the canaries? And the guinea pigs?"

"I sold them. Or traded them at a profit. You know what Dad always says—'Another day, another dollar.'"

"Well, I don't care what you do with all your different pets," Mrs. Sharpe said, "as long as you don't let them dirty up your room."

I was too stunned to move. *Never had a pet in his life*? Why, apparently he had never had anything *but* pets! Could this mean the other things he'd told Freddy had been lies as well?

"What did the mouse cost you?" Mr. Sharpe asked. "Did you trade, or was it cash on the barrelhead?"

"Neither," said Aubrey. "I just talked to this kid for a while, and finally he was so dumb he gave it to me for nothing."

Aubrey's father laughed. "A chip off the old block. Before long you'll be teaching your old man a few tricks!"

He drew out a roll of twenty-dollar bills and handed one to his son. "I had a pretty good week myself," he said, "so go out and buy whatever you want. Now I'm heading into the living room, and I'd like some quiet for the next couple of hours. I'll be watching football on TV."

At the sight of all that money, my head seemed to spin. Bankrupt, was he? Lost his money, had he? And what about the police, and jail, and Aubrey going off to an orphanage? All lies, I realized now, told to work on poor Freddy's warmhearted sympathy, to swindle him out of his pet.

A feeling of dismay crept into my bones. What sort of boy *was* Aubrey? What kind of troubles was I faced with? The more I thought of my situation, the darker it became. I had fallen into unscrupulous hands, and instinct warned me that I'd be lucky to survive.

7

"OH, SAD IS THE MOUSE!"

It did not take me long to suspect that Aubrey was a wicked owner indeed. The first day, he placed me far away from the window.

And he neglected me in a number of ways. He rarely cleaned out my cage, and he never gave me fresh water to drink until the dish was nearly empty. When a film of dirt settled across the surface, he didn't notice it—or didn't care.

My diet was meager and scarcely fit to eat. Every now and then I received a small, hard lump of foul-smelling turtle food left over from the previous residents. There were no more delicious hazelnuts or cashews, no slim wedges of Liederkranz or Brie like the ones Freddy used to slip into my cage.

At no time did Aubrey show me any affection. He did not think of me as a sensitive companion, brimming over with life, but merely as a useful piece of property, to be disposed of at the earliest convenience and at the best possible price. My only hope was that he would trade me, and quickly.

The most difficult thing to grow accustomed to was the solitude. Except during the cleaning woman's weekly visit, the door of Aubrey's room remained shut from the time he left for school in the morning until his return in the late afternoon. With little or nothing to interest or divert me, I moped around for hours at a time.

I suppose it was only natural that I thought a good deal about the past. As I paced up and down to get some exercise, I recalled the cheerful, carefree days at Freddy's place. How I wished that I might return to his apartment—and that I'd never heard of Aubrey Sharpe III!

I thought of my sister, too, and wondered how she had fared since we parted. Was she happy now? Had the little girl proved to be a kind owner? Did she treat Anna with the same consideration that Freddy Willis had shown to me?

Driven by loneliness, I decided to take up a hobby. I remembered some of the poems I had heard in the pet shop, and I began to make up rhymes and verses of my own. Of course the things I composed were not particularly clever. I knew that if the Parrot had heard them, he would have said with towering scorn, "Not in the same league with the work of the Master!" And I was sure the Hamster would have dismissed them with a curt "Dreadful doggerel, Christopher! Totally unworthy of serious criticism!"

Yet they permitted me to amuse myself, and sometimes they helped relieve my feelings. One that I liked was called "Oh, Sad Is the Mouse!" It went like this:

> *Care and despair*
> *Are everywhere!*
> *Gloom and doom*
> *Waft through the room!*
> *Oh, sad is the mouse,*
> *In his small, cardboard house!*

For his owner, alas,
Is a snake in the grass!

Oh, unfortunate mouse!
Oh, miserable mouse!
Oh! Oh! Oh!

It was full of self-pity, to be sure, but it was a comfort all the same.

At night, instead of being alone, I had Aubrey for company. After supper he sat at his desk and did his homework. With that accomplished, he leafed through his trading cards, for he did a thriving trade at school in those popular items. Then he emptied out his pockets and put all his cash on the desk. Dollar bills went into one pile, coins into a second. Quarters, dimes, nickels, and pennies were stacked in turn. Finally he added them up and announced in a triumphant voice, "Sixteen dollars and twenty-three cents today! Profit: twelve dollars and sixty-nine cents! Capital gains for the week: forty-seven percent!"

As he was counting his money one evening, the

telephone rang. He picked up the receiver and said, "Yes, this is Aubrey. Freddy? That's mental telepathy—I was just going to call you!"

Curious to learn what he would say, I trotted across the cage and pressed my ear against the bars.

"No, I'm afraid things haven't been too good," Aubrey began. "You remember, I told you he was *very* old. Still, I did what I could. I followed your directions—cleaned out his cage, just the way you said."

"Liar! Liar!" I muttered.

"Of course, Freddy. Every day he had one hazelnut and one cashew, and every other day a slice of Brie—"

"I never did! I never did!" I cried.

"—but nothing really seemed to help. I could see him growing steadily weaker. Today, when I got back from school, I found him lying there on his side, all curled up, his little eyes closed. I touched him, but he didn't move. He was dead!"

I gnawed the bars with exasperation. Dead? Me? Never! How could he tell such a tale?

"Yes, I'm sure he died peacefully. Animals generally do when they're his age. Well, as soon as I saw he was dead, I took him right over to the park and buried him under one of the cherry trees, so that every spring, in May, the blossoms will fall on his grave."

Aubrey paused. I saw him frown. "I'll tell you why, Freddy. I didn't call you before I buried him because I thought the funeral would upset you too much if you went there with me. I know how you loved the little fellow—and believe me, in the park, I did everything just the way you would have liked it. I buried him in an empty box of kitchen matches, and I said a brief prayer over his grave. It was beautiful, I think. . . . No, Freddy, no, *don't* thank me. I only did it for a friend. . . . I'll miss him too, especially if I end up at the orphanage the way I might."

After saying good-bye, Aubrey came over to my cage. "For a dead mouse, you look like you're in pretty good shape," he said with a grin. "And you'd better stay in shape! Because one day some stupid kid will come along, and I'll get rid of you for a fat price. Yes, sir, you crummy little mouse, you're as good as money in the bank to me!"

I found it difficult to sleep that night. Long after

Aubrey had turned out the light and begun to snore, I paced around inside the darkened cage. I tried to soothe myself with the thought that he would soon trade or sell me, and that from then on my fortunes were bound to improve.

Still unable to sleep, I crawled into my cardboard house and began to compose a new poem. My brain was throbbing; inspiration came in a flood. The words poured out, till finally I had finished it. I called the poem "Ode to Aubrey."

> *I hate you, Aubrey Sharpe the Third!*
> *You're a scoundrel, through and through!*
> *When you fall sick, you have my word,*
> *I'll waste no tears on you!*
>
> *And on the day you sell me,*
> *I will jump around with joy*
> *For I need no one to tell me*
> *You're a wicked, wicked boy!*

I said it over several times, changed a word here and there, and shut my eyes. I thought that even the

Parrot might have liked it, and that the Hamster might have said, "You're getting closer to *real* poetry, Christopher."

One afternoon the door opened, and the cleaning woman came into the room. As there was nothing else to do, I watched her straighten out the desk, sweep under the bed, and run the vacuum cleaner over the carpet. She had never spoken to me before, but this time she looked into my cage and said with a shudder, "Aren't you an ugly thing! Mice are so creepy-crawly! I wouldn't have you in *my* house for all the tea in China!"

Well, as my friends at the pet shop had often said, it takes all kinds to make a world, so I didn't allow her remarks to unsettle me. I shrugged coolly and thought, *She finds me ugly, does she?* And *I'd* always assumed that I was reasonably handsome and attractive. Not too clever, perhaps, and certainly not remarkably courageous, but still a rather appealing figure. However, everyone's entitled to her opinions, I suppose.

The cleaning woman said nothing more to me. She had finished straightening up and, with a final look around, dragged the vacuum cleaner out of the room. After a few moments her footsteps faded down the hall.

For a while I rested on the floor of my cage and tried to decide how to pass the time now that she was gone. I could always close my eyes and take a nap, or scrape off some mildew and have a nibble of turtle food. Or maybe try to get some exercise, by doing a hundred paces up and down. . . .

To my surprise I saw that the door of the room was standing ajar. It had never been left open before. While I watched, it seemed to move a little, as though something—or someone—was cautiously edging it open.

I went over to the side of the cage and looked out with a growing sense of uneasiness. Sure enough, the door moved again. This time I was certain of it. *How extremely odd*, I thought. *Who could be coming in here this way?*

As I peered out of the cage, I felt my heart stop. Standing in the doorway was the mortal enemy of every mouse in the world: a cat, huge and black, with pale green eyes and deadly velvet paws.

8

DESPERATE CIRCUMSTANCES

I froze, panic-stricken, at the bottom of my cage. The cat turned and looked inquiringly around the room while the end of his tail twitched in the most sinister way. Then he stalked silently across the carpet between the table and the bed until he was lost from view.

Remaining motionless so that he wouldn't hear me, I tried to regain control of myself. *Be calm, be calm!* I kept repeating. *Things will work out, Christopher, if only you don't lose your head!*

Gradually I became less agitated. My position, though grave, was far from hopeless. The cat had no idea that I was in the room, and he might not discover my presence. Even if he did, I would still be safe, for my cage was perched on top of the table. How could he possibly hope to scale such a height? And there was the cage itself. Surely if the bars had been strong enough to resist my gnawing teeth, they would prove strong enough to resist his tearing claws. For the first time since the door had opened, I was able to draw a deep breath.

My sense of tranquility did not last long. In a few seconds I saw the cat directly below me, staring up at the cage. He had discovered me. Now he was searching for a way to reach the top of the table.

I lost sight of him again. In the silence, I trembled with dread. Could he somehow reach me? Could he actually be strong enough to jump so high?

The answer came quickly. Hearing a faint noise, I turned to find him poised on top of Aubrey's desk.

All that separated us now was the space between the desk and the table. He meant to get across at a single bound. Crouching low to gather his strength, he lashed out furiously with his tail. Then he sprang. For a moment I thought he had missed and fallen to the floor. I was mistaken. I saw his forepaws clinging to the table and heard a scratching sound as he hauled himself up. When he drew nearer, I detected a sharp odor I had never experienced before. It filled me with disgust; I realized it was the odor of a cat.

He sat down a foot or so away and looked at me. He didn't speak, but I understood what he was thinking. *White mouse, I've come to get you,* his expression said. *I shall take you out of your cage and amuse myself. I'll pretend to let you escape, and you'll dash here and there in a desperate effort to elude me. Just when safety seems within reach, I'll drag you back and you'll have to start again. After a while, when I've grown tired of our game, I'll pounce on you for the last time, and kill and eat you—white fur, long whiskers, and all. However, I see I have a small problem to deal with first. How shall I get at you inside that cage?*

Slowly he rose to all fours and drew closer. I shrank back to the opposite side of the cage and watched him as he delicately flicked out one of his paws and tested the bars. He hooked them with his claws and gave a sharp tug. They held firm, and he let them go.

He paced in front of the cage while I continued to shrink away. He tested the side, the top, the front. Each time, to my relief, the bars remained unyielding. Finally, putting out a paw, he tugged savagely at the door of the cage. It, too, held firm.

He settled on his haunches and thought some more. Just as I was beginning to hope that he might have given up, he rose to his feet and returned to the back of the cage. I wondered what he planned to do. Would he try the bars again, or did he have a new scheme in mind?

Imperceptibly at first, the cage began to slide across the table. In a flash I realized what was happening. Another few seconds and the cage would pitch over the edge and plunge to the floor. Possibly the force of the fall would loosen some of the bars so that he would be able to pry them apart—far enough apart to reach inside and seize me.

He shoved steadily with his shoulder against the back of the cage. The floor teetered and swayed under my feet until, with a sickening lurch, over I went. Down I fell, to land with a jolt in a pile of paper shavings. At the same instant, there was a terrific *crash*, and the dishes broke, cascading dirty water and turtle food across the carpet.

I scrambled to my feet and saw the cat leap down from the table. He had eyes for nothing except the overturned cage. He reached out and tested the bars, one by one, but they remained undamaged. He couldn't budge them. Apparently his scheme had failed.

Only it hadn't. I saw something that had escaped his notice. The door of the cage—its tiny hinges had been loosened. A few strong tugs and the door would fly open, and I would be left to the tender mercies of my enemy.

Shutting my eyes, I huddled in a corner and prepared for the end. I could feel the cage shake as he pried at the door. Confused memories swept through my mind. I seemed to hear my mother saying—as she had once at Mrs. Crimmins's place—"Never despair! How much worse the situation could be!"

Except that *my* situation couldn't have been worse! I was cornered. There was no hope of escape. Soon he would drag me out . . . and I would run . . . and he would pounce. . . .

I stopped, puzzled by something. The cage was no longer being shaken. I opened my eyes. The cat had turned away and was staring with amazement at the door of the room. He must have heard a sound I missed. Then I heard it too—rapid footsteps in the hall. The door flew wide and in stormed Aubrey, his face contorted with fury.

He had come back from school in time to hear the dishes breaking. Fortunately, he hadn't been delayed on his way home. A few minutes more and he would have been too late to save me.

The cat didn't find it fortunate, however. He let out a shriek and leaped aside as Aubrey aimed a kick at his ribs.

"Get out of here!" my owner screamed, and for a single second I thought of him as a kindhearted boy after all—a fine boy who was horrified at the fate I had so narrowly avoided.

His next words dispelled the illusion. The cat dashed past him in an effort to reach the safety of the hall, and Aubrey aimed another kick and shouted, "Rotten brute! What were you trying to do in here—eat up my capital assets?"

Afterward he returned the cage to the table, filled a new dish with water, and gave me a teaspoonful of turtle food to replace what had been lost. When he left to eat his own supper, he shut the door of the room with great care.

This act of caution failed to reassure me. I suppose the next hour was one of the darkest of my life. I knew that I was still in terrible danger, for Aubrey hadn't noticed the damage to my cage. Sooner or later the cleaning woman or someone else in the household would leave the door of the room ajar, and the cat would slip in. A few seconds and he would wrench my cage open and finish me off.

After supper Aubrey sat at his desk, took out an empty box of kitchen matches, and began to bore holes in its sides. I heard him whistling, a sign that always meant he was pleased with himself. When the holes were finished, he pushed the box aside and looked at me.

"You're coming with me to school tomorrow," he said. "I'm not taking any more chances. Before the family cat gets in here and kills you, I'm going to make a fast deal with one of the kids. I've got the right sucker picked out already. So why wait? How much can I sell you for once you're dead?"

At these words—callous as they were—a vast weight seemed to lift from my heart. Soon I was to be traded or sold. I would belong to someone else, and *any* new owner, I was sure, was bound to be an improvement on Aubrey.

Which merely proved how much I still had to learn about life.

9

THE BOY WITH THE STUFFED OWL

The next morning I left for school in a cheerful frame of mind. What difference did it make if the box of kitchen matches was dark, cramped, and poorly ventilated? A brief farewell inside, and then *adieu* forever to Aubrey Sharpe III!

There was a rule against bringing pets to school, and this made Aubrey cautious. He refused to exhibit me, but at each recess he threw out tantalizing hints to his classmates about the "fabulous bargain" concealed in his desk drawer.

"I've got just what you're looking for!" he said to various customers. "Meet me in the locker room before gym."

"Okay, Aubrey, meet you in the locker room," they replied.

The day passed slowly—various classes, lunch in the cafeteria, more classes, and finally gym. Aubrey didn't feed me. What did he care? I'd soon be sold, and that would be that.

Downstairs in the locker room Aubrey took me out and put me on his arm. The response was disappointing. Only two of the boys seemed interested in having a white mouse, and the others drifted away.

One of the two made an offer. "I'll give you a dollar," he said.

"Not enough," said Aubrey.

The other boy said, "Let me hold him," and Aubrey handed me over. I sat on the boy's fingers and saw him smile. He reminded me of Freddy Willis. I felt sure he was the one I wanted.

"I'll pay you a dollar fifty," he said. "I'd like to stuff a white mouse with my new taxidermy set. Last week I stuffed a dead owl and he came out fine. Of course I'd have to kill this one first, but I don't guess that would be any trouble. I could use an anesthetic, or poison. What do you say, Aubrey? I'm looking for another specimen."

Aubrey's horror apparently matched my own. "Sell my pet to a taxidermist?" he said. "Sell my white mouse to someone who plans to kill and stuff him? I may need money pretty badly, but I don't see how I could sell him to *you* at any price."

Unabashed, the Youthful Taxidermist offered a dollar seventy-five. The other boy went to two dollars, claiming it was his top price. The Youthful Taxidermist said he would pay two dollars and a quarter, and he might throw in some of the duplicates from his baseball card collection.

Aubrey bit his lip uncertainly and told them he would need more time to reach a decision. "We can decide tomorrow," he said. "I need cash, sure—but there's a moral question. I mean, do I accept the best offer and sell my pet to somebody who's going to murder him in cold blood? Or do I stand by my principles and take less money on the deal?"

I understood Aubrey well enough to know that he was playing them against each other, but which one was "the sucker" he had in mind? It *couldn't* be the Youthful Taxidermist, whose radiant smile had reminded me for a moment of Freddy— and whose real character had proved to be so different.

It was early evening by the time we reached home. Aubrey whistled happily as he returned me to my cage. "I thought it went pretty well today," he said to me. "I've got him hooked. He can hardly wait to buy you. Then you can join the stuffed owl on top of his bookcase. Won't you look fine there!"

I crept into my cardboard house and lay still, too stunned to move. I should have guessed that his talk about principles and moral questions had been the merest pretense. He *was* going to sell me to the Youthful Taxidermist! Without a qualm, he was going to place me in the hands of a boy who would butcher me! Truly there were depths of wickedness in Aubrey that even *I* had never suspected.

Several hours later the idea came to me. Aubrey, his homework finished, went to the kitchen for a snack. He brought back a sandwich and a glass of milk and stood near my cage. "After a real hard day," he said, "there's nothing like a peanut butter and jelly sandwich! Here, have a piece, you stupid mouse—might as well enjoy yourself while you can."

A peanut butter and jelly sandwich . . . where had I heard of that before? What did it remind me of? At Mrs. Crimmins's place . . . my mother telling Anna and me a story . . . about a traveling salesman . . . and how her great-uncle Julius had escaped. . . .

Escaped! Of course! He'd *escaped*! And if Great-Uncle Julius had been able to, why couldn't I?

The plan I made was a simple one. I could see no point in trying to break out of my cage—the family cat would be waiting for me down the hall. I would have to escape at school, or in some other place, while Aubrey was carrying me around in his pocket. That day, he'd shut the matchbox tight each time. But people do make mistakes, grow careless, and if Aubrey did, I'd be ready for him.

The next afternoon, instead of going to gym, Aubrey and the other boys and girls ran downstairs and jumped into the school bus. Our destination, announced the teacher, Mr. Bloodworth, was the Metropolitan Museum of Art.

The one boy had dropped out of the bidding, and when the bargaining began again with the Youthful Taxidermist, I paid no attention until I heard Aubrey say, "Let's get it straight. You'll give me two seventy-five, your desk globe, and your duplicate baseball cards—and I mean all of them—and then I'll give you the white mouse."

"Okay, all my duplicates. Can I have him now?"

"No, later. After school. We'll go down to your place and make the trade."

"Well, at least let me see if he's still in good condition, Aubrey. I need a perfect specimen. If he's gotten damaged since yesterday, the deal's off."

"How could he get damaged?" Aubrey said. "He's in terrific shape. Here, take a look if you want." He removed me from the box and put me on his sleeve.

Two girls were sitting on the other side of the bus. I must have startled them. They saw me and let out several shrieks.

"Hey! What's going on back there?" Mr. Bloodworth shouted. "Sharpe, are you making trouble again?"

"I haven't done anything, sir!" Aubrey said. He

THE BOY WITH THE STUFFED OWL 95

hurried me back into the box.

"I'm warning you. Sharpe, if I have to speak to you once more this week, you're going to wind up in the principal's office! And I promise you, if that happens, you won't like it!"

The threat flustered Aubrey. He slipped the box hastily into his pocket—but this time he failed to shut it tight.

When I was sure he wasn't thinking about me, I pushed gently against the drawer. It slid open a little farther. More important, Aubrey hadn't noticed what I was doing. I was so light that he couldn't feel me through his coat. I pushed again. Soon the opening was large enough to let me out whenever I wanted. I crouched down and waited.

The bus trip over, Mr. Bloodworth steered the children to the museum auditorium. The class took seats. I could hear a woman speaking. She told a joke about Egypt and the long-dead pharaohs, but no one laughed. After that she said, "Please turn out the lights," and she began to talk about the Pyramid of Cheops.

Aubrey and the Youthful Taxidermist exchanged

"playful" punches on the arm. As the woman droned on, they giggled and called each other names too vile to repeat. Aubrey's attention was certainly not on me.

It was now or never. With infinite caution, I eased my way out of the box.

Inch by inch I climbed the lining of his coat pocket. A single misstep would cause me to fall, and the commotion would foil my escape. Fortunately, I didn't slip. Before long I was safely at the top, and I poked my head out to look around.

At the front of the auditorium I could see a faint glow of light. The rest of the room was in darkness.

The next moment I was tiptoeing down the back of the theater seat to the floor. There I paused for breath. Somewhere above me in the dark Aubrey Sharpe III wriggled and punched and swore. I had been lucky. He didn't have the slightest idea what I was doing.

I paused again to gain another breath, and then I hurried away from the light toward the rear of the auditorium. Freedom and safety were within my grasp.

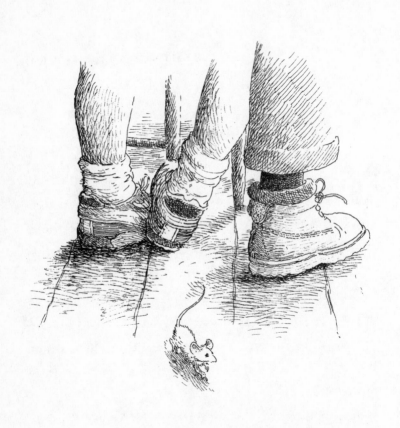

10

SOMETHING OVERHEARD

The first hazard to face me was the children's feet. Aubrey's classmates were scattered across a dozen rows, and there was no telling when one of them might become restless and stand up—right on top of me.

Zigzagging around the boys' and girls' shoes, I soon left the danger zone behind. I raced under empty seats toward the exit; everything was quiet while I ran, so I knew I had avoided detection thus far.

I stopped near the glowing EXIT sign. A mouse can squeeze into the narrowest crack, and I saw plenty of daylight beneath the double doors. Which course should I follow? Would it be wiser to remain in the auditorium and hope that nobody would see me after the lecture was over? Or should I hunt outside for a hiding place, where I could stay till the children had gone? I decided to risk a peek at the corridor.

Squirming beneath the doors, I emerged on the other side. At first I was dazzled by the light and failed to notice a man walking toward me. The stone floor shook under his tread. Before I could heed the warning, he came striding by, his feet so close that I could see the flash of his purple socks and the polish gleaming on his shoes.

I looked around hastily and saw paintings on the walls, pieces of sculpture along the corridor, and, across the way, a long blue sofa. It was unoccupied—a perfect place to hide. A glance left and right told me no one else was coming.

"Ready! Set! Go!" I said and scurried over the floor, up the side of the sofa, and under the nearest cushion. I was hidden—and safe at last!

Relief flooded through me. I wasn't going to be sold to the Youthful Taxidermist! I wasn't going to join the stuffed owl on the bookcase! I was going to live, to breathe fresh air and enjoy the sunlight, to munch happily on cheese and nuts for years to come, to laugh and make jokes, to dance and sing. . . .

Behind the cushions I curled up into a comfortable ball. Maybe I should have begun to draw up future plans without delay, but I didn't. The occasion called for rejoicing. My friend the Parrot had told me once, "When the Poetic Muse arrives, welcome her!" She arrived while I was hiding in the museum sofa and filled my brain with a storm of words and rhymes. The lines tumbled out, and in no time I had finished a poem of triumph. I called it "The Mouse Who Copes!" This is the way it went:

Come and listen to my story,
If you care for tales of glory,
For the dangers I encountered were immense!

My best weapons, while I battled,
Were strong nerves that never rattled,
And a dash or two of simple common sense!

Oh, my turtle food was wormy!
I was faced with taxidermy!
But my mouse's heart remained as firm as steel!

I refused to knuckle under,
So it's hardly any wonder
That with every mounting crisis I could deal!

When I lost my owner, Freddy,
I relied on courage steady
To escape from Aubrey Sharpe, that wicked boy.

Soon I tiptoed from his pocket,
Sped to safety like a rocket,
And felt overcome with happiness and joy!

Now I rest in idle splendor,
Filled with gratitude most tender
For the way good fortune favored all my hopes!

In the future, never doubt it,
Rodents everywhere will shout it—
"There goes Christopher—the little mouse who copes!"

I was still polishing a few of the final lines when the children came out of the auditorium. "The museum closes in twenty minutes," Mr. Bloodworth told them. "Everyone's free to go home, or to come with me and look at the mummies and statues of the pharaohs in the Egyptian Wing."

I could hear the children shuffling away, some in this direction, some in that. Then the sofa shook violently as somebody sat down. At the same time, the metal springs let out a painful *twang* right next to my ears.

The person above me didn't stir. Footsteps drew nearer. I heard a girl say, "Why are you sitting there, Aubrey?"

Aubrey replied, "I lost something important."

The sofa shook and the springs went *twang* a second time. "What did you lose?" she asked him from the next cushion.

"My white mouse. It must have been on the bus. Or here in the museum."

"Can't you buy another one?"

"I was going to sell him for a big price today. Now the deal's off. And I've already told my dad about it. Will he laugh! And call me stupid too!"

"Does he care that much? I mean, if you get a lot of money or not?

"That's all he *does* care about. How much *he* makes—and my learning to be as smart as he is."

"Why tell him, then?"

"I guess I won't. I'll make up a story. I'll say I got five dollars for the mouse, and after that maybe he'll let me alone for a while."

A bell rang in the corridor. "I think they're starting to close," the girl said. "Here comes one of the guards."

"I'll walk with you, if you're going east."

"Okay," the girl said. The sofa shook and there were two more *twangs* as she and Aubrey stood up and moved away.

Several alarms were ringing now. The corridor grew noisy as more and more people came walking by. "Please move to the exits," the guards kept saying. "The museum's closing . . . museum's closing. Please move along."

I decided to wait till the building was locked up before coming out. Probably a few guards would be on duty at night to protect the museum's treasures, but I felt sure that I could avoid being seen.

Because I no longer had an owner, I would have to provide for myself. I would need a supply of food and water and a place to sleep. At some point I would have to take stock of things and make permanent plans.

I wondered how long it might suit me to remain on my own. Suppose food was plentiful, and I found no difficulty establishing a snug nest in some secluded corner of the museum. Why not remain indefinitely? If living conditions were comfortable and safe, why bother to find a new owner?

Maybe I'd stay on my own forever. Quite possibly a free and independent life was the one for me!

My impatience mounted as the minutes ticked away. The alarms had stopped ringing. The corridor grew still. A man walked slowly along, humming to himself—a guard, I supposed. He stopped by the auditorium doors. I heard a key turn in the lock. Soon his footsteps faded in the distance.

After a long spell of silence I crawled out of my

hiding place. Most of the lights had been switched off. At one end of the dark, empty corridor a single bulb glowed. Outside, beyond the tall windows, the night was black.

Despite the gloom I set off with a jaunty stride. The stone floor felt slippery and cold beneath my feet. I found dust along the walls. Large clumps of it had gathered in the corners, and some got into my nose and made me sneeze.

I paused from time to time to look at various paintings in their gilt frames and pieces of sculpture on their pedestals. The atmosphere was not ideal for admiring works of art. The rooms were too dark and sinister; the entire building seemed deserted.

I turned a corner and entered the Egyptian Wing. Heavy stone tombs stood everywhere, their sides covered with carvings of strange birds and animals. The statues of the long-dead pharaohs faced one another across a little courtyard, and a tremor of dread shook my limbs as I hurried between them. The statues looked as if they might come to life at any moment, those ancient kings, seated on their high marble thrones.

How lonely it was, how utterly still. I looked around and listened; nothing could be heard. I ran ahead until I came to a hallway, where I saw a window with a shaft of moonlight pouring through it. The night was getting on. Cheered by the brightness, I trotted forward.

Suddenly I stopped in my tracks.

On the floor, a few feet away, there was a shadow. The shadow of a gigantic cat!

I was in desperate straits—out in the open with no hole to race to, no crack into which I could dive. Escape was impossible. One leap from his perch and he would have me.

What stupidity—running about in plain sight! How mad, how insane not to have been more careful! Of course a museum was just the sort of place a cat might be lurking!

It's not easy to account for what I did next. Perhaps my life with Aubrey had changed me, had taught me more tricks than I realized. Instead of dashing away in panic, I coughed politely and said in my suavest voice, "Look, friend cat, before you finish me off—and I know you can do it whenever you please—why not consider a business proposition?"

His silence seemed encouraging. Apparently I held his full attention. I couldn't see where he was sitting, but I noticed that his shadow hadn't moved.

"Suppose you eat me at once," I went on briskly. "What do you stand to gain? A brief snack, a couple of swallows—that's all it will amount to. But suppose instead you spare my life, and we go into partnership? Have you thought of the benefits from such an arrangement?"

He didn't answer—didn't even nod his head. I found this disconcerting. What was his plan? To let me talk myself out before jumping down and converting me into his supper?

"There are so many things I can do for you!" I cried. "Here's an example: I'll provide you with a life of leisure! Let me tell you how it'll work. You'll sleep all night, and I'll be your lookout. Whenever I see one of the guards coming, I'll wake you up, and you'll be able to run around and make a terrific impression. They'll say you're the best museum cat they've ever had, and you'll grow fat, dining on the extra treats they'll give you!"

Not a word did he say in reply.

"Or suppose," I continued desperately, "some enemy decides to poison you! You must have heard of cats being poisoned; it happens all the time. But not to you! Not after we're partners! Because I'll be your personal food taster! I'll sample everything first, and if there's poison in your food, *I'll* be the one to die . . . with a smile on my lips, knowing that you spared my life, and that finally I was able to repay my debt to the dearest friend a mouse ever had."

Silence, only silence.

My eloquence had failed. My scheme had been futile. I hadn't deceived him. All I could do now was gather my courage, say a last prayer, and wait for the dreadful moment when he would pounce.

11

ON MY OWN

Minutes passed, yet the gigantic shadow didn't move. I couldn't understand why. Was it possible he hadn't heard me? A deaf cat guarding the museum? That hardly seemed likely. Could he be napping? No—cats never went to sleep sitting up.

Whatever the explanation, I began to suspect he didn't know I was there. I took a cautious step, and then another. When nothing happened, I drew a breath. Counting to three, I dashed away and flung myself into a dark corner. I looked back. The shadow hadn't stirred.

It was very strange. He acted as if he were made of stone. A new thought struck me: suppose the shadow didn't belong to a *living* cat. . . . I left the corner and ran along the wall till I had a full view of the room. In a moment the mystery became clear. My enemy was seated within a glass exhibit case, high on a pedestal in the moonlight. According to his placard, he was an ancient Egyptian cat, a prize museum statue—and more than two thousand years old.

What a humiliating discovery! Imagine making such a stupid mistake! I was glad no one had witnessed my performance. Eager to put the entire incident behind me, I crept down the corridor and out of the Egyptian Wing.

At first I moved ahead slowly and stayed close to the walls. I had grown accustomed to the darkness and no longer felt apprehensive on that account. I feared two other possibilities: a live cat might be somewhere in the museum, or I might stumble into one of the guards.

Eventually I grew bolder again. If the museum *did* have a cat, I would have discovered some evidence of him by this time—a trace of his scent or some of his hair in one of the corners. Since I hadn't, it seemed safe to assume that no cats were about. As for the guards, I quickly lost my fear of them after meeting two or three who were making their rounds. They had eyes only for the paintings and statues and didn't bother to shine their flash- lights on the floor. If I kept alert and out from underfoot, I saw no reason why they should notice me.

Back and forth I prowled through shadowy cor- ridors and galleries. I'm not sure when I discovered how hungry I'd become—and how cold. The stone and concrete floors were bad enough; the museum was also drafty. Every now and then I ran into a gale that seemed to blow out of nowhere; it swirled along the hall for a few seconds and then abruptly died away, leaving my teeth chattering and my long, furless tail as chilled as an icicle.

Shortly after one of these freezing blasts, I stopped to rest. I was standing in front of a black door. A sign said MEMBERSHIP OFFICE. Could there be any food inside? The next moment I was wrig- gling through the crack above the sill.

The office was dark except for a patch of

moonlight on the carpet. I saw a number of pieces of office furniture: filing cabinets, a leather sofa with three cushions, two desks, and an overstuffed chair. I climbed the sofa and searched it. No food had fallen behind the cushions. I tried the chair without success. A desk was next; using the wall to keep from falling, I shinnied up to the top of it.

Suddenly a glorious scent tickled my nose. It was the rich, redolent aroma of roasted peanuts! Someone in the membership office enjoyed a snack between meals—and the desk drawer had been left open!

I plunged down and soon found seven peanuts in a bag. I fell to work. In no time I tore a hole through the cellophane. I gnawed away and finished all seven.

My hunger satisfied, I paused to reflect. I hadn't had a drop to drink since early morning, and the salted nuts had made me even thirstier. There was another reason to move on. I needed a safe place to sleep, and staying in the desk drawer would certainly be too risky.

On the other hand, I was weary after my day's

adventures. The nerve-wracking escape from Aubrey and the hours I had spent exploring the museum had left me exhausted.

Sleep was stealing over me. I decided to compromise. First I'd take a short nap; later on I'd go out and search for water and a more suitable place to hide.

I saw a package of tissues at the back of the drawer. Extracting two sheets, I dragged them over to a corner. When I had fluffed them up, I had a small but luxurious bed.

My eyes slid shut. With a sigh of contentment I curled up and lowered my head. A moment later I was fast asleep.

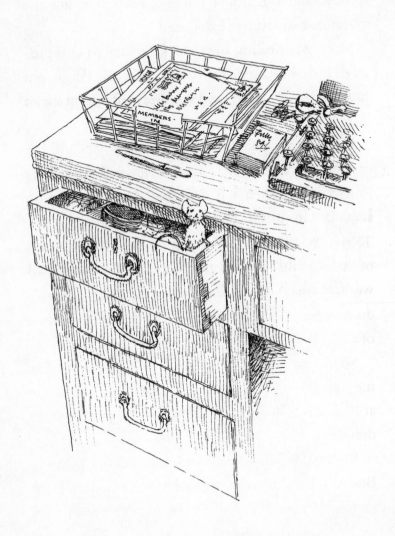

12

LIFE AMONG THE LADIES

I awoke to hear a variety of noises around me. There was the rustle of papers, the clicks and hums of nearby office machines. Above my head two women were discussing what they had eaten for dinner the previous evening and the new shoes one of them had worn to work that morning.

Suddenly I leaped to my feet. I had overslept! The membership office was open, two of the ladies were at their desks, and I was trapped below in one of the drawers!

My first impulse was to rush out and flee to safety. But in what direction did safety lie? I had only the sketchiest idea of the office layout. A single wrong turn might land me in an even worse predicament.

I decided to be patient. Eventually the ladies would grow hungry. In time they'd go to lunch, and I could make my escape while the office was deserted.

I resigned myself to waiting. My hunger had returned, yet I felt no desire to eat; by now my thirst had become so strong that I could think of little else except the need to satisfy it.

Finally I heard the lady at the other desk push back her chair. "I'm going to the restaurant before the crowd arrives," she said. "Want to come along and get something to eat, Amelia?"

"No thanks, Cordelia," the lady at my desk replied. "I've got too much work piled up. On your way back, would you bring me a sandwich?"

So Cordelia went to lunch, Amelia continued working, and I remained inside the drawer, still unable to escape without being seen. I tried to distract my mind, to think of something beside water: my escape from Aubrey, the episode with the Egyptian cat, my other museum adventures. Maybe I could make something useful out of the past—create some verses to guide young mice of a future generation, when they left home to face the world.

The lines came slowly. Was ever a poem composed under more trying circumstances? I persisted, however, and in time the work was done. I called it "Christopher's Advice to Younger Mice." This is the way it went:

> *A traveler's life*
> *Is filled with strife—*
> *Don't try it, you'll regret it!*

> *Footsore you'll roam,*
> *Without a home—*
> *I urge you to forget it.*

> *With woe and rue*
> *You'll wander through*
> *Vast buildings dark and dreary.*

> *From dust you'll sneeze.*
> *From drafts you'll freeze,*
> *Your four legs stiff and weary.*

For food you'll pine
While others dine.
For water you'll grow frantic.

At dead of night
You'll flee in fright
From shadow cats gigantic.

Ah, rash young mice,
Heed my advice!
My sermon do not sleep through!

If you should find
An owner kind—
Delight him so he'll keep you!

While reciting the lines, I couldn't help smiling. How invaluable such advice would have been to me when I was younger—and how little chance that I'd have taken it.

As the afternoon wore on, a new idea suggested itself. Suppose Amelia liked white mice. Might she be interested in having me for a pet? It was true that I wasn't looking my best. The general abuse I'd suffered for such a long time at the hands of Aubrey Sharpe III had left my coat a bit dirty and my glorious whiskers sadly drooping. Nor had the events of the last twenty-four hours improved my appearance. Nevertheless, I still possessed my native charm and an instinctive talent for pleasing any sensitive human being—or so I believed.

Perhaps the soundest plan would be to emerge from the drawer and casually introduce myself. If Amelia liked me, she could take me home and my troubles would be over. There was another possibility, though. What if she didn't care for mice? I'd come popping up from nowhere with a cheerful smile and a flick of my tail—and all too likely set off a small-scale disaster.

I was trying to decide what to do when the drawer shot open. I saw a woman's hand reach in and grasp the cellophane wrapper.

"Good grief, Cordelia, will you look at this? I had at least two dozen peanuts, and they've all been eaten!"

"Seven, lady, *only* seven," I muttered. "Don't exaggerate."

"Let's see, dear. Why, that bag's been gnawed right through. It looks like a mouse did it!"

"A mouse?" cried Amelia. "I hate mice! I hope we don't have any in here!"

"I hope we don't!" cried Cordelia. "I hate mice too!"

Well, so much for that. No home with Amelia—or Cordelia. And I'd have to stay hidden till they departed for the evening.

The next moment Amelia put her hand against the drawer and slammed it shut.

Would she open the drawer again before leaving? She *had* to. My throat was so parched already that if I were forced to spend the night without water, I could hardly hope to survive!

I made a decision. If she *did* open the drawer, I was coming out. Before she could shut it a second time, I would seek safety in flight, no matter how grave the risks.

Overhead, the two ladies went on typing. I heard Amelia say, "It's only four-thirty," and Cordelia reply, "Yes, Friday always seems like the longest day of the week, doesn't it?"

Friday! My doom was sealed. The odds were a hundred to one the office would remain shut over the weekend. I could never last through all of Saturday and Sunday. My only chance was to escape while they still were here, and in less than half an hour they would leave!

Just when I was ready to abandon hope, the drawer shot back open and Amelia thrust in a huge pile of papers. "Finished at last!" she said. "I never thought I'd get the job done!"

The papers were so bulky, they wouldn't fit without being forced down. The drawer was open a crack. I hurried over, stuck my head through, and peered around.

Amelia was standing up. Her back was half-turned. She was gazing critically at her shoes. I lurched up, scrambled out of the drawer, and dived under the desk.

She remembered the papers and returned to the desk. Pressing them down, she shut the drawer. Then she turned a key and locked it. A few seconds' delay and it would have become my tomb!

Even so, I was not safe yet. At any moment she might look under the desk and see me huddled there.

Hoping their eyes would remain elsewhere, I dashed across the open space to the sofa. My scheme was simple: burrow under one of the cushions, stay in hiding till the ladies departed, then leave the office by squirming under the door.

At that point my luck gave out. Cordelia spotted me as I mounted the sofa, and she let out a scream.

"What's the matter?" cried Amelia.

"I just saw the mouse!"

"Where?"

"Over there! He went under the cushion!"

There was a menacing pause. I heard Amelia say, "*He's cornered*! Where's my umbrella? I'm going to find him and finish him off!"

I was about to conclude that Amelia was the most thoroughly unsatisfactory woman I'd ever encountered when I heard Cordelia say, "I'll help you! Get my umbrella too! Hurry up, Amelia!"

There was no time to lose. I sped along the back

of the sofa, under the cushions, to the opposite end. I made a ninety-degree turn, ran to the front, and poked out my nose.

The ladies were bending over, a few feet away. They had lifted the first cushion. With a shriek they began to thrust their umbrellas into the sofa.

"Where can he be?"

"Look under the next cushion!"

"We've got him trapped—don't let him get away!"

Taking advantage of the pummeling they were giving the sofa, I slid to the floor and headed full speed for the door. I was halfway there when it opened. In came a third lady, carrying another pile of papers.

"Say, what's going on in here?" she asked.

"A mouse!" cried Amelia and Cordelia together.

"In the museum? Nonsense! How could there possibly be—"

At that moment she looked at the carpet. Her jaw dropped; her hands flew up. The papers shot away in all directions. As they floated to the floor, she screamed, "There he is!" I bolted between her feet, and the museum alarms went off.

I fled through the open door. A single glance told me I'd chosen a poor time to come out of hiding. The corridor was filled with people; crowds of visitors were streaming toward the exits.

I kept to the walls, racing against the human tide. Now and again, when it couldn't be helped, I dashed across an open space. At every step of the crossing I expected to be squashed underfoot.

I heard a hubbub behind me.

"Did you see the mouse?"

"No, where?"

"There he goes! He went around the corner!"

Footsteps were pounding after me.

Straight ahead was a door marked MEN. I ran over and squeezed underneath. The shouting grew fainter.

I'd stumbled into a washroom. There was a radiator against the wall. I trotted over and ducked behind it. Before long the door swung back and two museum guards came in.

"You see the mouse in here?"

"No, I don't see a mouse. He must have gone

somewhere else."

The door shut; the corridor outside grew still. My heart began to beat more calmly. The day was over; soon the museum would be closed, and for a while, at least, I would be safe.

13

WEARY TRAVELER

When I was sure the danger had passed, I came out. I could think of nothing but water. A row of porcelain washstands rose high above my head; I scaled the radiator to have a look.

Three of the gleaming bowls were dry, but not the last. Someone had failed to shut off the faucet completely. It was dripping slowly—the first water I'd seen in two days and a night.

Half mad with thirst, I hurled myself down the side of the slippery bowl. Skidding as much as running, I reached a point under the faucet, opened my mouth wide, and tilted back my head.

Drop by lovely drop, the water fell between my

parched lips. Greedily I swallowed each one, and just as greedily I waited for the next to fall. Finally, I managed to drink my fill.

I tried to climb back out—and discovered I couldn't. The porcelain was too smooth; it offered nothing for my feet to grip. By dashing full tilt I could get partway to the top, only to come sliding helplessly down again.

After several futile attempts I paused to rest. I had never been in greater peril. Undoubtedly someone would come to the washroom soon to tidy up and would find me struggling in the bowl.

It was odd, but instead of panic I felt only a sense of resignation. How difficult it was for a white mouse to survive on his own. I'd been free for scarcely twenty-four hours, and already I was exhausted by my efforts to escape destruction. Enough food and water and a safe place to sleep—the simplest things needed to sustain a creature's life—how hard they were to obtain. Looking up at the rim of the bowl, such a short distance above my head and yet so inaccessible, I was tempted to wait there and accept my fate.

A thought crossed my mind. My mother's great-uncle Julius had been found in a jar of jelly, and here *I* was, trapped in similar circumstances. Was it a family weakness? Was I the victim of an inherited tendency to get into hopeless corners from which there was no escape?

I refused to believe it. I would *not* suffer the fate of Great-Uncle Julius! One way or another I was going to get out!

Something caught my eye as I glanced around. I looked again. It was a discarded paper towel. The top end reached almost as high as the rim of the bowl. If it would bear my weight without slipping, it might provide me with a ladder to safety.

I stepped gingerly on the bottom end. It was damp and stuck to the slippery porcelain beneath. I backed away and gathered my remaining strength. Running as lightly as I could, I rushed along the length of the towel. At the very last moment I leapt upward and clawed my way back to the rim.

After that I didn't pause. I hurried down the radiator and left the washroom by way of the door.

My thirst had been satisfied, but now I began to

feel fierce pangs of hunger. I remembered Cordelia's mentioning a restaurant in the museum, and I set out to find it.

Once more I wandered through dark rooms and windy corridors. Then I saw a sign that revived my hopes. RESTAURANT, it said in bold letters. Beneath it was an arrow pointing the way.

I hastened down another corridor and through an unfamiliar gallery. At last I came to the restaurant itself, filled with tables and chairs. Hundreds of museum visitors must have dined there earlier in the day. Surely there would be some scraps lying about.

I searched everywhere, patiently, but in that great dining hall, the only thing I found was a single crumb of bread.

Utterly disheartened, I wandered into the pantry, where I saw two tall doors. Standing back, I realized what they were guarding: a mammoth refrigerator. Behind those doors were cakes and cookies, juices and sodas, cheeses of every sort, and quite possibly a few pounds of mixed nuts as well—enough food to maintain an army of white mice for an entire century.

I could never hope to squeeze beneath those doors. They were fitted perfectly. There was not the slightest space between them and the sill. Nor was there a hole or crack anywhere in that unassailable fortress. I made sure of it. I sat down, put my head against the refrigerator wall, and gave way to tears.

I don't know how long I remained in the pantry. Eventually, as it was growing light outside the museum windows, I dragged myself away. I went back through the dining room and into a small gallery crowded with ancient statues and vases.

A heating pipe stood against the wall. I crawled behind it and lay down on the floor to sleep.

Soon it would be daytime, and visitors would begin to arrive at the museum. I had already decided what to do. When I awoke, I would leave my hiding place and approach the first person I saw. If he liked me, he might take me home to be his pet. If he didn't, that would be the end of Christopher.

There was no other choice. I had learned that I couldn't hope to survive on my own. Either I would find a new owner, or I would perish swiftly. In either case, my torments would be over.

14

WALTER AND ABBY

I overslept again. When I awoke, it was to see the midday sun streaming across the gallery floor. Its brightness did nothing to cheer me. Wracked anew by thirst and hunger, I rose to my feet and looked out from behind the heating pipe.

The gallery was almost deserted. A young woman sat in a folding chair, sketching a vase. Farther off, a tall man stood before one of the statues, his back to me. No one else was in the small room.

I didn't know which stranger to choose. The young woman was only a few feet away. She would be easier to reach, but would that be wise? My success with ladies hadn't been outstanding lately.

What if she were another Amelia-Cordelia? Should I make the extra effort and approach the man on the other side of the room?

No. I was too weary to take a single unnecessary step. It *had* to be the woman. At least I could see one favorable omen: she didn't have an umbrella among her possessions.

With a coolness born of desperation, I came out and tottered toward her chair. She didn't see me at first. I edged closer. After a moment she glanced down and gave a start.

"Well, hello there," she said. "What in the world are *you* doing here?"

She seemed completely unflurried. I took a few more steps, but not quickly enough to frighten her.

"I'll bet you're lost," she said. "And probably hungry. So don't run away. Just sit there while I see if I haven't got something for you to eat."

She needn't have worried—running away was the last thing I had in mind.

I watched her reach into the large canvas bag beside her chair and fish out a package of cheese-flavored crackers. She broke one up and put the pieces on the floor. Crawling over, I began to wolf them down. It wasn't easy—they were extremely dry and I could have done with some water—but I gave no sign that liquid refreshment might be needed as well.

I moved toward her again. I was desperately anxious to make a good impression, yet I knew that my bedraggled appearance worked against me. Still, I held my head as proudly as I could and tried to keep my whiskers from drooping too much.

She turned and called out softly to the man by the statue. "Walter, don't come running and frighten the creature, but look what's here!"

Walter walked across the gallery and stopped nearby. "I'll be darned!" he said. "Where did you find him, Abby? Imagine—a white mouse in the Metropolitan!"

"He just came wandering by," she told him. "I'm sure he's somebody's lost pet. He's quite tame. Half starved too—you should have seen him eating the cracker I gave him."

"Slim pickings here, I guess."

"I think we should keep him," she said. "I've got a box we could carry him home in. The children would love to have him. What do you think, Walter?"

"Why bother to ask?" he said. "Suppose we didn't. You'd tell the Smith children how their father kept them from having a white mouse, and I'd end up in the doghouse for a month. Okay, I'll try to catch him for you."

I sat back and waited while Walter took out his hat and explained to Abby how he was going to slip up behind and snare me in it without doing any damage to my delicate constitution.

My capture was effected quickly. I didn't budge as he dropped the hat over me, wrapped me up in it, and swooped me aloft.

"Here's the box," Abby said. "It's got plenty of holes, so he won't have trouble breathing."

Moments later I was safe inside the box. I heard them packing their things; when all was ready, Abby put me carefully into the canvas bag, and we left the museum and went out to their car.

My spirits soared. What a fabulous stroke of luck

finally had come my way!

As we drove off, Walter said to Abby, "You'll need something to keep him in, won't you?"

"Why not a cage?" Abby replied. "Maybe we could buy one in that awful-looking pet shop near the supermarket."

They began to talk about their three children, who were spending the weekend in the country with Abby's mother. When the children returned, Walter said, they'd be delighted to find a pet—a white mouse, rescued under such spectacular circumstances from the art museum.

I learned that their oldest child, Claire, was fond of animals. She would be put in charge, and the twins, Philip and Lucy, would receive their instructions from her. It sounded like an admirable arrangement, and I felt certain that I was in perceptive and intelligent hands.

When we entered the pet shop, I heard the tinkling of a bell and couldn't help wondering if we were stopping at Pete's. Any doubts were dispelled when Doc's voice boomed out from the back of the store. "What can I do for you folks? Tropical fish? A puppy? Kennel supplies?"

"We're looking for a cage to keep a white mouse in," Abby told him. "We found the poor thing in the museum, and we don't know anything about cages."

"I've got exactly the thing you want!" Doc said. "By sheer coincidence, there's a special on cages this month. Here is one that would be perfect for a white mouse. Let me see the price—only forty-nine ninety-five!"

"A *special*?" Walter laughed.

There was a pause. "You think the price is too high? Well, I *could* be mistaken—I'll look at the tag again."

Another pause followed. Doc coughed and said, "Say, you're absolutely right! I apologize for my mistake. This cage *was* forty-nine ninety-five—but for this week only, just seven days, it's marked down to twenty-nine ninety-five. Can you believe it—I didn't see where the numeral 'four' had been changed!"

The sale was made, and the shop bell tinkled again. We got into the car, drove to the street where

Walter and Abby lived, and climbed to their apartment.

My new owners did well by me. They padded the floor of my cage with clean paper shavings, transferred me into it, and set out a slice of Limburger for my lunch.

I fell on it savagely.

"Wow—it looks like he's starving!" Walter said. "I'll cut off another slice. I didn't know a mouse could eat so fast!"

And Abby said, with a marvelously intuitive understanding, "I'll bet he's thirsty too. Mice must need a good deal of water. I'll put some in a dish for him."

By nightfall I had settled comfortably into my new quarters. Tired but content, I prepared to rest. For the first time in weeks I felt free of anxiety. No danger threatened. I was back in a cage, placed there by two kind owners—and after the experiences I'd had on my own, I didn't mind the confining bars a bit.

I grew drowsier. My thoughts wandered. I made up some new lines . . . for what? . . . to go with a tune instead of humming it . . . a traveler's song, to be sung after a long and perilous journey. . . .

> *Christopher nests in peace tonight.*
> *His past was dark—his future's bright.*
> *His yesterdays were filled with sorrow.*
> *His happiness begins tomorrow.*

15

There was great excitement the following evening when the children returned from the country. They crowded around and stared at me, the twins, Philip and Lucy, standing on tiptoe to see into my cage. Claire was a head taller. She opened the wire door and took me out, and I sat on her hand. Though I didn't itch, I scratched myself to amuse them. It sent them into shouts of laughter.

"I want to hold him!" Philip said.

"We'll take turns," Claire told him. "But when you do, Phil, you've got to be careful not to squeeze too hard, because you could hurt him."

"I'd be scared to hold him," Lucy said. "He might

try to bite me."

"White mice don't bite," Claire said. "They're tame and gentle. Look—is he biting me now?"

A sensible, well-informed girl. I could tell I was going to like Claire. The twins, however, promised to be different. I wondered whether they weren't too young and inexperienced to handle small pets, namely me.

At any rate, their older sister was in charge and I was glad of that. Getting to my feet, I walked sedately up the sleeve of her dress. She smiled and said, "Isn't he wonderful?" That's when I knew we were going to get along famously.

I crawled across her shoulder and gave her cheek a friendly rub. She giggled, and I continued around her collar and down the other sleeve. Lucy said, "I guess I won't be afraid."

Philip said, "When can *I* have him?"

Claire put me down on the coffee table. "All right," she told him, "it's your turn." He grabbed me, picked me up—and squeezed!

If his older sister hadn't been watching, it would have been the end of me. His pudgy hand drove all the air out of my lungs; I saw stars; my eyes bulged from my head.

"Stop it! You're doing it too hard!" Claire cried. "Set him down, Phil!"

He put me back on the table, and I lay still. Was I alive—or dead? Had he crushed every rib in my body—or merely bruised them? I tested things, and I found I could breathe all right, and that no bones had been broken. But I'd be sore for a week!

"He's hardly moving," Claire said. "He must be badly hurt."

"I think you've killed him," Lucy said. "You were too rough, Philip. You always play too rough."

"I didn't mean to hurt him," Philip said. "I just wanted to hold him. Why doesn't he get up?"

I had a flash of inspiration. This was the time to make a firm impression on the young boy—to put on a performance he would never forget. I lay on my side and gave my tail a pitiful twitch. I raised my head, only to let it fall back on the table. I kicked my legs out in three dramatic spasms—and went limp.

"He's dying!" Claire said.

"You've killed him!" Lucy screamed, and she

burst into tears.

"I didn't mean to, I *didn't*!" Philip shouted. Then he began to howl louder than his sister.

Well, enough was enough. I seemed to have gotten my point across. I raised my head again and struggled gallantly to my feet. I staggered a few steps, paused, and staggered on.

The children gasped. There were shouts of "He's alive!—He's up!—He's walking!" and I could tell from the relief in their voices that my act was a success. Nobody in the Smith household was going to squeeze me too hard again.

My life soon settled into its current routine. Each morning now, Claire looks after my cage. She gives me fresh water and new paper shavings and sees to it that I have enough nuts and cheese and other good things to eat. Under her tender, loving care, my health has been restored: my white coat has regained its glossy sheen; my whiskers have recaptured their former resiliency.

Weekends and early evenings I devote to the children. They let me out of my cage for exercise,

and I walk around on their hands and arms. Philip
has learned to be more gentle, and Lucy no longer
fears that I'll nip her finger. I do my best to amuse
them. I run up and down the furniture, chase my
tail, and perform various exotic dances when they
put music on the CD player. They laugh, clap their
hands, and call me charming names that I feel are
not totally undeserved.

During the daylight hours I divide my time
between the cage and the drawing board. Walter
and Abby are both hardworking artists; they bring
me over when they feel like taking a break, and I
stroll among the inkpots, the scattered pencils, and
the India rubber erasers. I'm becoming more familiar with their skills. Sometimes they let me
approach their drawings and sketches so that I can
see what progress they've achieved. Abby is
strongest with watercolors and gouaches; Walter is
the better draftsman—I've heard him say so himself.

The other day I got into the green ink by mistake. Were they disturbed? Not in the least. Walter
said, "I think he's got some talent. Let's see what he
can do, Abby." He dipped my feet into different inks

and placed me on a clean sheet of paper. I weaved about in all directions, till finally the sheet was covered with mouse squiggles. That night they showed my painting to a few of their friends. Someone said the galleries would soon be bidding for my work.

It's a pleasant life, and one that I thought would never change. And then, earlier this week, I began to feel a bit listless. I sneezed a few times and ran a slight fever. Nothing to be concerned about. I knew it was merely a virus I'd picked up from the children.

The family noticed I wasn't my usual self, though. Abby said I must have eaten too much. Walter thought it was artistic exhaustion, stemming from overwork. Lucy declared I was dying, and Claire said the radiator was too hot for me and moved the cage away from it, toward the center of the room.

Philip said, "I think he's lonely. He needs a friend. Let's get another white mouse to keep him company."

Everyone was enthusiastic about the idea, except for me. My feelings were mixed. An unfamiliar mouse around the cage might be an annoyance. He could turn out to be someone who enjoyed late-night snacks and kept me awake till all hours with his gnawing and gulping. He might be selfish and try to hog the paper shavings, or be untidy and put his feet in the water dish.

On the other hand, it would be pleasant to have someone to chat with. I could listen to whatever adventures he'd had, and he undoubtedly would be delighted to hear about mine.

After school today, Claire came bursting in with the news that she had stopped at the pet shop. They had one white mouse in stock. Could she go over tomorrow morning and buy it? Walter and Abby said yes, there was no reason why she couldn't.

Claire's next words gave me a jolt. Apparently the white mouse in question is a Retread! Doc told her as much. He said he'd sold it to a little girl a number of weeks ago, but the girl grew tired of the mouse and brought it back the other day.

Of course the idea is absurd! I recognize that. After all, I'm a realist now.

But Doc *did* sell my sister, Anna, *to a little girl a number of weeks ago.* . . . What of it? To a *fickle* child, whose mother said at the time, "Angelica Rose, dear, you know how you're always changing your mind. Are you *entirely* sure you want a white mouse?"

Absurd—completely absurd. A city like New York must be filled with fickle little girls who grow tired of their pets and return them. It must happen all the time.

I won't be in suspense much longer. A few more hours and it will grow light outside. The children will go to the pet shop and return with a shoe box—I do hope Doc doesn't charge them for it— and Claire will take the Retread out. . . .

Who will it be? It *could* be a perfect stranger. Someone to talk with now and then, someone who will make things more lively here.

I have such an odd feeling in my bones, though—a feeling that it might not be a stranger after all. It's only a hunch, I know, but something tells me that it could be my sister at the pet shop, and that our story might end the way every story should, with singing and laughter—and a poem that says that after our long separation, Anna and I lived happily ever after.